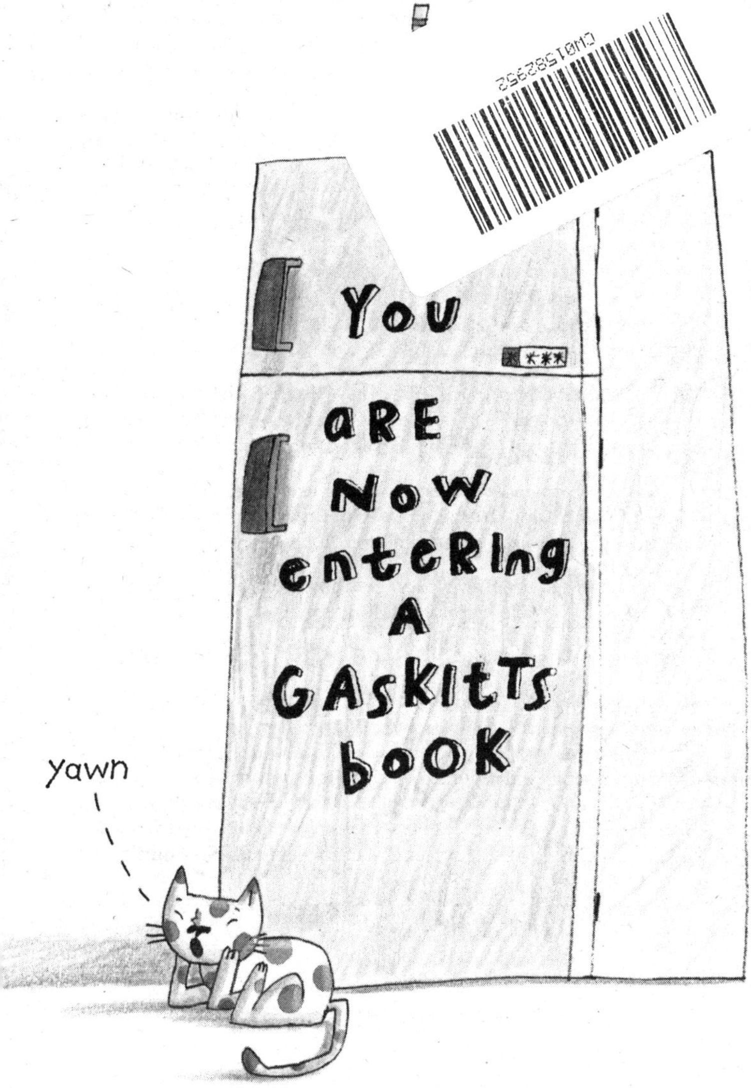
YOU
ARE
NOW
ENTERING
A
GASKITTS
BOOK
yawn

This is a work of fiction. Names, characters, places and incidents are either the product of the author's imagination or, if real, used fictitiously. All statements, activities, stunts, descriptions, information and material of any other kind contained herein are included for entertainment purposes only and should not be relied on for accuracy or replicated as they may result in injury.

First published individually as *The Man Who Wore All His Clothes* (2001), *The Woman Who Won Things* (2002), *The Cat Who Got Carried Away* (2003) and *The Children Who Smelled a Rat* (2005) by Walker Books Ltd
87 Vauxhall Walk, London SE11 5HJ

This edition published 2026

2 4 6 8 10 9 7 5 3 1

EU Authorized Representative: HackettFlynn Ltd,
36 Cloch Choirneal, Balrothery, Co. Dublin, K32 C942, Ireland
EU@walkerpublishinggroup.com

This book has been typeset in Stempel Schneidler Std, Cafeteria, ElaTapioca and Kosmik

Printed and bound by CPI Group (UK) Ltd, Croydon CR0 4YY

British Library Cataloguing in Publication Data: a catalogue record for this book is available from the British Library

ISBN 978-1-5295-3306-4

www.walker.co.uk

FSC
www.fsc.org
MIX
Paper | Supporting responsible forestry
FSC® C013604

ALLAN AHLBERG

THE MAN WHO WORE ALL HIS CLOTHES

AND OTHER STORIES

ILLUSTRATED BY

KATHARINE McEWEN

WALKER
BOOKS

Contents

The Man Who Wore All His Clothes

Contents

Meet The Gaskitts

Mr Gaskitt

A slim young father who sometimes wears all his clothes.

Mrs Gaskitt

A loving mother and hard-working taxi-driver.

Gus and Gloria Gaskitt

Nine-year-old twins.

Horace:
the Gaskitts' Cat

Likes easy chairs,
old movies on TV
and cat food ads.

The Gaskitts' Refrigerator

Five-star freezer,
large vegetable
compartment,
good speller.

The Gaskitts'
Car Radio

Sometimes gets
things wrong.

Chapter 1
Mr Gaskitt Gets Dressed

One morning in the month of December

Mr Gaskitt got up.

He put on his vest and pants and socks,

and his socks and vest and pants,

and his pants and socks and vest.

"Lovely socks, dear," said Mrs Gaskitt.

He put on his three shirts and

his two pairs of trousers.

"Very smart, Dad," said Gloria.

He put on four jumpers and a tie.

"Great tie, Dad," Gus said.

Meanwhile, Horace had jumped into Mr Gaskitt's still-warm bed.

All of a sudden, the phone rang.

"I want a taxi," said a gruff voice.

"Right," said Mrs Gaskitt. "When for?"

"In half an hour – on the dot."

"Right," said Mrs Gaskitt.

"Where from?"

"Pick me up outside the bank," said the voice.

"Right," said Mrs Gaskitt. "And where will I take you to?"

"As far away as possible," said the voice.

"Only joking lady!" and he hung up.

Mr Gaskitt ate his breakfast.

He put on his jacket,

his anorak,

his overcoat,

his three scarves,

his two pairs of gloves

and his plastic mac.

"Don't forget

your hats, dear,"

said Mrs Gaskitt.

Mr Gaskitt kissed his wife and children –

"Goodbye, darlings!"

"Bye-bye, Dad!"

– and left the house.

Chapter 2

Mr Gaskitt Gets Stuck

Mr Gaskitt squeezed into his car.

A little snow had begun to fall.

He switched on the radio.

I must get that radio fixed,

thought Mr Gaskitt.

He drove down the road,

round the roundabout

and up and over the flyover.

He stopped at the traffic lights:

red – amber – green.

Meanwhile, Horace
had come downstairs
and was watching TV
in the sitting-room.

Mrs Gaskitt
was parked
outside the bank.

Gus and Gloria were at school

watching – Oh no! – their poor old teacher

falling down from a ladder.

The teacher's name was Mrs Fritter.

She landed with a dreadful bang,

got a big lump on her head and

had to go home.

Back in the car, Mr Gaskitt was stuck in the traffic.

A lorry had tipped over while trying to reverse.

"STAND CLEAR!

I AM REVERSING!

BEEP, BEEP!

I AM STILL REVERSING!

BEEP!

I AM SKIDDING!

I AM FALLING OVER!

BEEEEP!"

Now the lorry's load of Christmas trees

was rolling around all over the street.

The lorry itself was lying on its side.

Mr Gaskitt sighed and
twiddled with his radio.
"The roads are clear,"
the radio said.
"No hold-ups anywhere.
A happy Easter to all
our listeners."

Chapter 3
Mr Gaskitt Gets Going Again

The road was clear and the sun was shining.

Mr Gaskitt was on his way again.

"Terrible traffic jams," said the radio.

"Fog everywhere!

Eat Mrs Mossop's mince pies."

Mr Gaskitt stopped at the petrol station.

He got: 4 free wine glasses

3 car stickers

2 cans of Slugg

1 packet of Protts

a giant economy bag of popcorn –

oh yes, and some petrol.

Meanwhile, Horace had left the house and was visiting a friend.

Gus and Gloria were getting into trouble with the supply teacher, whose name was Mr Blotter.

The problem was,

Mr Blotter had not taught for many years.

His ways were somewhat …

… old-fashioned.

BANK

Meanwhile also, outside the bank

Mrs Gaskitt was getting impatient.

Just as she was about to leave – Bang! –

out of the bank rushed a small man.

He had his collar turned up and

his hat turned down.

He was carrying an enormous bag.

"Where to?" said Mrs Gaskitt.

"Er, the airport," growled the man.

"Shall I put your bag in the boot?"

"Er, no."

The man clutched his bag and

looked over his shoulder.

"I'd rather hold on to it."

Chapter 4
Mrs Gaskitt Smells a Rat

Mr Gaskitt was driving along.

"Soon be there now," he said to himself.

The radio was playing a rock 'n' roll song.

Suddenly a voice said,

"We interrupt this rock 'n' roll song

with a newsflash:

THERE HAS BEEN A ROBBERY AT THE BANK!"

"Fancy that," said Mr Gaskitt.

"THE POLICE ARE ON THE LOOKOUT

FOR A BAD MAN WITH A SMALL BOG,"

said the radio.

"NO, ER, A LARGE
MAN WITH A BAD
BACK. A
SMALL BAG
WITH A …
OH, DEAR."

Mrs Gaskitt had her radio on too.

"Wow, a robbery at the bank!" she cried.

"Dreadful," growled her passenger,

and he clutched his bag closer.

"You got out of that bank just in time,"

said Mrs Gaskitt.

"Yeah," growled the man. "Lucky, wasn't it?"

Just then a police siren began to sound

in the street behind them.

"Step on it," growled the man.

But Mrs Gaskitt was getting suspicious.

"Why should I?"

"Because I say so," growled the man.

Mrs Gaskitt smelled a rat.

"Wait a minute – what have you got in that bag?"

"Mind your own business,"

growled the man.

And he said,

"Turn left."

Meanwhile, Gus and Gloria were having more trouble with Mr Blotter.

"Fingers on lips!"

"Elbows on knees!"

"Left legs behind necks and over right shoulders!" said Mr Blotter.

Meanwhile also, Horace was at his friend's

house watching an old movie.

It was a sad old movie.

Horace had his hankie out.

Suddenly a voice said,

"We interrupt this sad old movie

with a newsflash:

THERE HAS BEEN A ROBBERY

AT THE BANK!"

Back at the school, the children

were setting off for the swimming-baths.

Mr Blotter was marching them

like soldiers on parade across the playground.

Meanwhile, out in the street

the bus was waiting.

School Bus

Chapter 5

Run Robber Run

Mr Gaskitt was still driving along and

his radio was still getting things wrong.

"THE ROBBER IS MAKING HIS GETAWAY

ON A MOTORBIKE," said the radio.

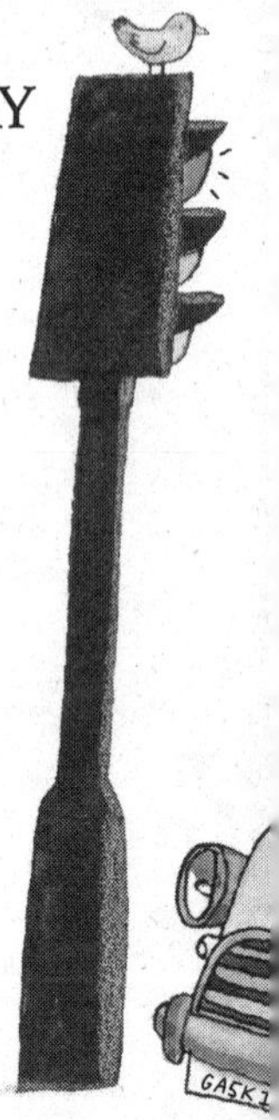

Meanwhile, the robber

was still in Mrs Gaskitt's taxi.

"THE ROBBER IS MAKING HIS

GETAWAY ON A FIRE ENGINE!"

yelled the radio.

Meanwhile, Mrs Gaskitt

had stopped at the traffic lights

and the robber had jumped out.

"THE ROBBER IS HIDING AWAY IN HIS

SECRET DEN EATING EGGS, CHIPS AND

BEANS!" hollered the radio.

Meanwhile, the robber

was wondering what to do next.

Just then he spotted the bus.

It was waiting at the traffic lights too.

Small round faces were pressed against the steamy glass.

One or two of them had their tongues out.

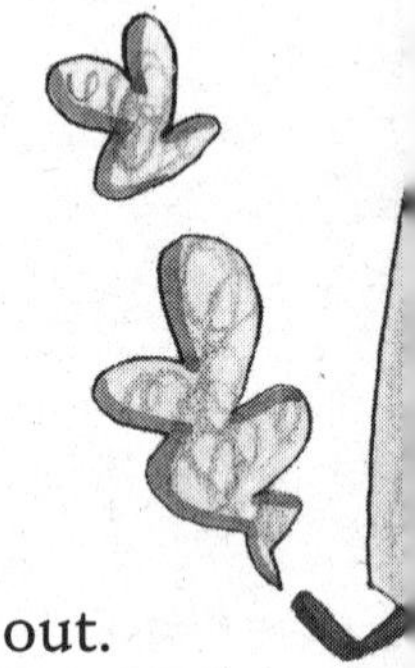

Meanwhile, Mrs Gaskitt was chasing the robber.

"Stop, thief!" she cried.

Down the street, the police siren was getting louder.

The robber opened

the door of the bus and jumped in.

Gus and Gloria were sitting on the front seat

with their swimming bags.

Mr Blotter stood up in the gangway.

"Who are you?" he said.

"Mind your own business," growled the man.

And to the driver he said, "Step on it!"

Chapter 6

"Miaow!" said Horace

Mr Gaskitt was

still driving

along.

Up ahead he thought he could see

Mrs Gaskitt's taxi.

Mrs Gaskitt was

running after the bus.

She thought *she* could see

Gus and Gloria.

Meanwhile, inside the bus Mr Blotter was asking, "What's all this? What's going on?"

And the children were telling him.

"It's a hijack, Sir!"

"A kidnappin'!"

"Ransom!"

"No, it ain't – it's a joke!"

"A trick!"

"He's pullin' our legs!"

Now the robber took charge.

From his pocket he pulled … a gun.

Well, a toy gun, actually,

the one he'd used in the bank.

"That ain't real!" yelled the children.

"I've got one of them!"

"It's plastic!"

"Silence!" growled the robber. "Blasted kids."

And he said, "Fingers on lips – hands on heads."

He was old-fashioned too.

Then to Mr Blotter he said, "And you!"

And to the driver, "Drive!"

DRIVE!
School Bus
SKOOL 4 YOU

The chase began.

The bus drove down the street.

Mrs Gaskitt in her taxi chased after it.

Mr Gaskitt in his car chased after her.

And the police chased after him.

And the *TV news reporter*,

with her TV camera man and her TV van,

chased after them.

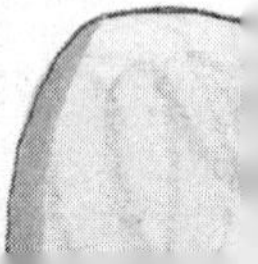

TV2000

Meanwhile, Horace was at his friend's house

watching TV.

It was a cat food ad for Crunchy Mice,

Horace's favourite food.

Suddenly, a voice said,

"We interrupt this cat food ad

for Crunchy Mice with live coverage of …

A POLICE CHASE!"

"Miaow!" said Horace.

Chapter 7

The Unhappy Robber

The bus went up the hill

and down the hill.

The children began

to whisper.

Into the underpass and out of it.

The children began to talk.

Round the roundabout

and up and over the flyover.

The children began to yell.

"Whee!"

"Please, Sir," (to the robber),

"I feel sick!"

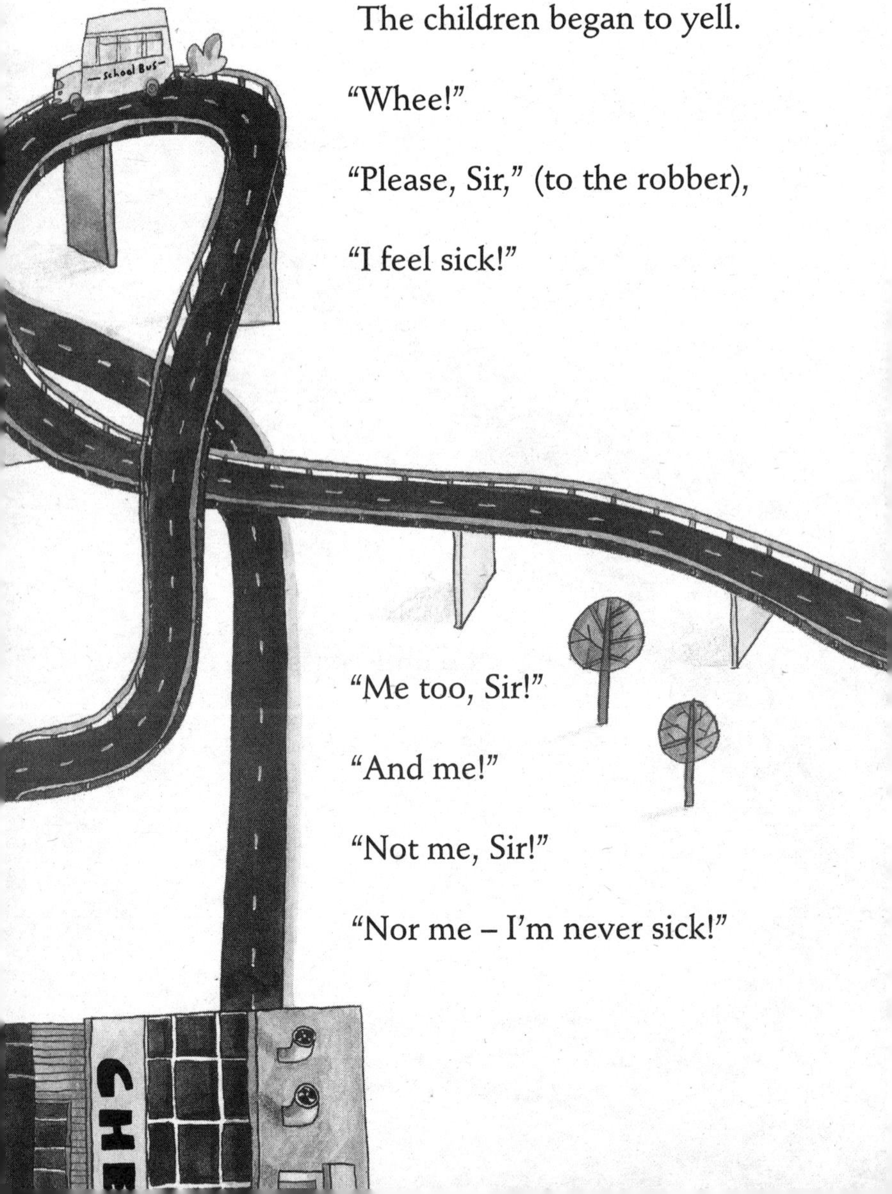

"Me too, Sir!"

"And me!"

"Not me, Sir!"

"Nor me – I'm never sick!"

“Silence!” growled the robber, but the children were now so noisy they couldn’t hear him.

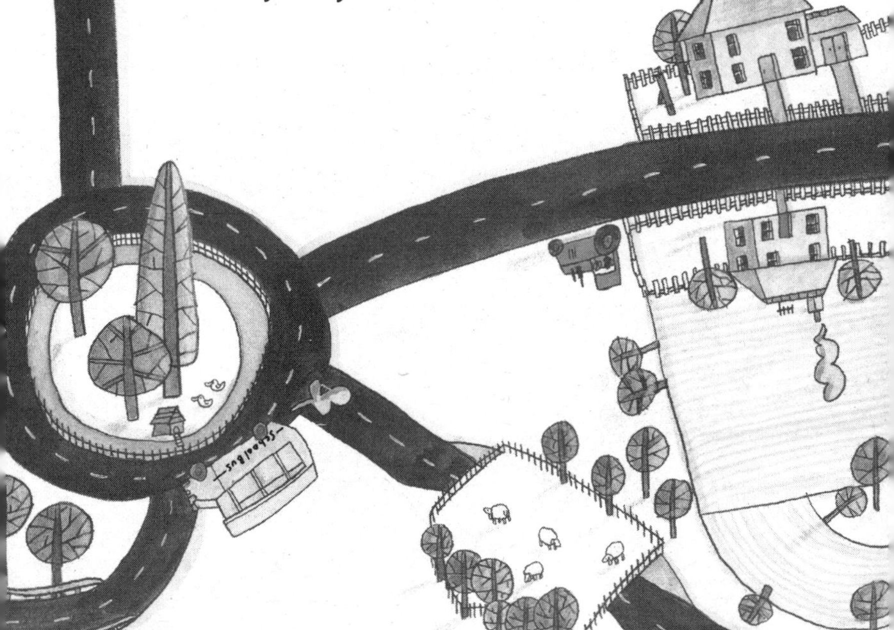

“Please, Sir, Tracey’s got my swimming goggles!”

“Jonathan’s got my towel!”

“Brian’s eating, Sir!”

“Are we nearly there now?”

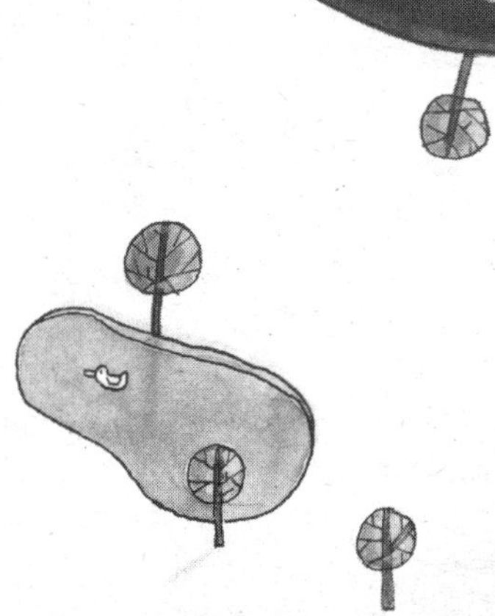

The robber felt trapped.

He put his hands over his ears.

This is worse than being in jail, he thought.

Meanwhile, Mr Blotter was smiling.

"*Please*, Sir!"

The noise grew louder still.

"Please, Sir!"

"He's got my—"

"Mr Robber!"

"No, I never!"

"Yes, you did!"

"That's not fair!"

"Mr *Robber!*"

"Stop pushin'!"

Meanwhile, "Mr Robber" was unhappy.

He looked out into the crowded, *peaceful* street.

And, "Stop the bus!" he cried.

Chapter 8

Mr Gaskitt Lends a Hand

Mr Gaskitt was *racing* along.

He was a worried man.

What was Mrs Gaskitt up to?

Why was she chasing that bus?

Mrs Gaskitt was also racing.

She was a worried woman.

What was that robber up to?

Where was he going with

Gus and Gloria?

Suddenly the bus stopped.

Out jumped the robber

closely followed by Mr Blotter,

the driver and twenty-seven children …

all yelling.

"Stop him!"

"He's gettin' away!"

"Tracey's got

my hairbrush!"

The chase began again.

The robber ran

into a supermarket

and out of it,

up an escalator

and down,

down an escalator

and up.

Into a lift,

and up and down

and up and down

and out.

Into a pizza parlour and –

Mmm – out, with a stolen pizza

(deep pan – family size – extra pepperoni).

The robber was little.

The robber was quick.

He twisted and turned

and ducked and weaved

and *nearly* got away.

The children couldn't catch him.

The police couldn't catch him.

Mrs Gaskitt couldn't catch him.

The robber ran out into the car park.

I'll steal a car, he thought.

"I'll get away. Mmm – this pizza's good."

Suddenly, there was *Mr Gaskitt.*

"Out of my way," growled the robber.

"No," said Mr Gaskitt.

"I may be little," growled the robber,

"but I'm hard."

The robber

tried to

run round

Mr Gaskitt,

but Mr Gaskitt

was too wide

for him.

He tried to

punch Mr

Gaskitt, but

Mr Gaskitt

didn't feel

a thing.

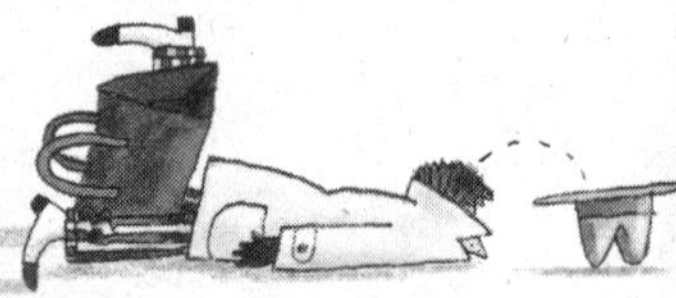

He tripped

over his own

enormous bag

and fell down flat.

Mr Gaskitt *sat on him*.

Chapter 9
What Horace Saw

Moments later, when the police

and the children

and the Christmas shoppers

and Mrs Gaskitt

and Gus and Gloria

and the TV reporter

(with her camera man and sound engineer)

arrived, all hot and out of breath,

there was the flat and captured robber,

and there was Mr Gaskitt,

cool and calm and eating pizza.

Then the police grabbed the robber.

Mrs Gaskitt hugged Gus and Gloria.

Mr Gaskitt hugged Mrs Gaskitt.

And Gus and Gloria hugged him.

Meanwhile, at his friend's house,

live on TV,

Horace saw it all!

"I know them!" he cried.

"No, you don't," said his friend.

"Yes, I do – they live in my house."

"No, they don't."

"Yes, they do – it's Mr and Mrs

and Gus and Gloria."

Horace purred with pride.

"I'm their cat."

Back at the car park

the police and the TV reporter

were asking questions,

and Gus and Gloria, mostly,

were answering them.

"He's our dad!"

"She's our mum!"

Mr Blotter was marching

the other children back to the bus.

The robber was on his way to jail.

There was talk of a reward.

Suddenly, Mr Gaskitt looked at his watch.

"Oh no!" he cried.

"Is that the time – I've got to go."

Mr Gaskitt kissed his wife and children –

"Goodbye, darlings!"

"Bye-bye, Dad!"

– and hurried off.

Chapter 10

Mr Gaskitt Goes to Work

Mr Gaskitt was driving along.

"Soon be there now," he said to himself.

He switched on the radio –

"ROBBER GETS CLEAN AWAY, POLICE BAFFLED!" – and switched it off again.

I really *must* get that radio fixed, thought Mr Gaskitt.

Mr Gaskitt turned left, drove past an automatic barrier,

and into a car park.

He squeezed out of

his car and hurried

into a lift.

Up went Mr Gaskitt:

first floor,

second floor,

third floor …

fourth floor.

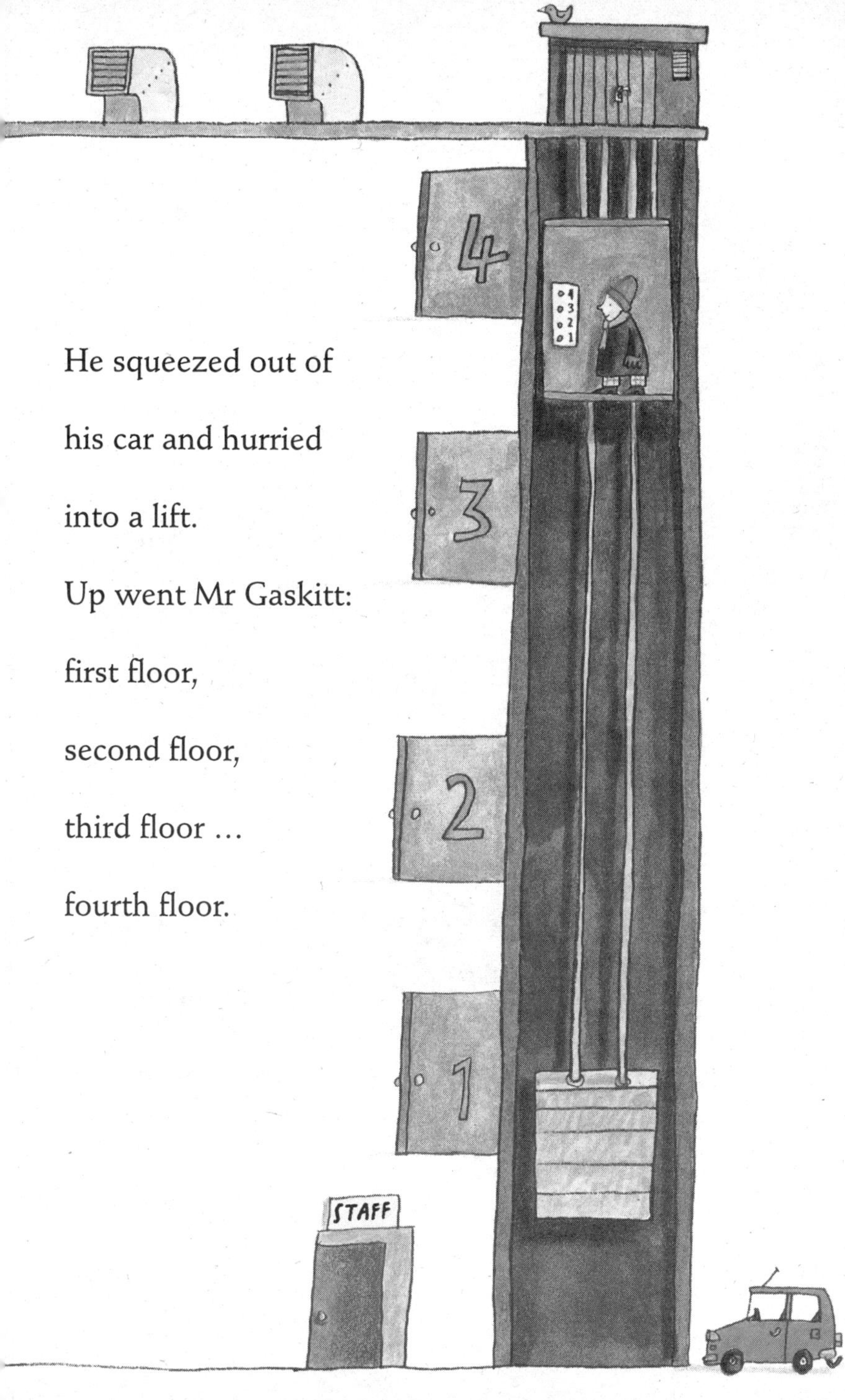

Mr Gaskitt entered a small room.

He grabbed the kettle

and made a quick cup of tea.

He looked at his watch.

What a rush! he thought.

Mr Gaskitt got ready.

He put on his red

working trousers

and his red

working coat,

his red working

hat and gloves,

his black

working boots

and his white

working whiskers.

"Ho, ho, ho!"

cried Mr Gaskitt,

and he went

to work.

Chapter 11

Mr Gaskitt Comes Home

Mr Gaskitt sat in his grotto

with children on his lap all day long.

He was the perfect Santa:

kind and *comfy*, like a big soft bed.

At half past five

Mr Gaskitt came home.

He took off his plastic mac,

his overcoat,

his anorak,

his jacket,

his three scarves

and his two pairs of gloves.

"Cup of tea, Dad," said Gloria.

He took off four jumpers

and a tie,

two shirts

and a pair of trousers.

"Evening paper, Dad," Gus said.

Mr Gaskitt sat in his chair.

He drank his tea and

read the paper.

"FATHER CHRISTMAS

SAVES THE DAY!"

said the headlines.

That evening the Gaskitts –

all four of them *and* Horace –

watched a sad old movie on TV.

They shared the popcorn,

wiped their eyes and waited …

for the happy ending.

Kitty
You
are
Now
Leaving
A
Gaskitts
Story
Bye-bye!

CRUNCHY MICE
STEP THIS WAY FOR ANOTHER GASKITTS STORY

The Woman Who Won Things

SEE YOU LATER HORACE!

Contents

Meet The Gaskitts

(and Horace's friend)

Mrs Gaskitt

A taxi-driver and loving mother who likes to enter competitions.

Mr Gaskitt

A fond hard-working father who always takes any job he can get.

Gus and Gloria Gaskitt

Nine-and-a-half-year-old twins.

Horace Gaskitt

A ginger-and-white cat
who likes to argue
with his friend.

No, I don't!
Yes, you do!
No, I don't!
Yes, you do!
No, I...
Yes, you...
No...
Yes...

Horace's Friend

A black cat
who likes to argue
with Horace.

The Gaskitts' Doormat

Mostly welcoming...

Sometimes grumpy...

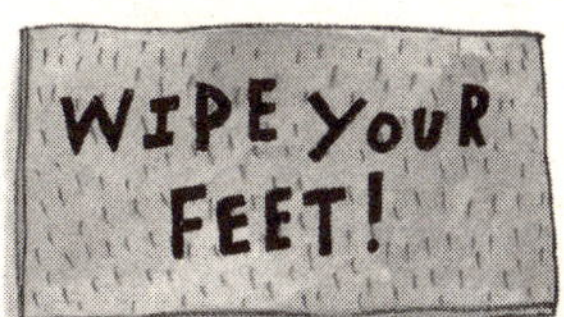

Sometimes rude...

Chapter 1
Mrs Gaskitt's Luck Begins

One morning in the month of May

Mrs Gaskitt got up.

She came downstairs, gave Horace a bowl

of Crunchy Mice

and gave his

friend one too.

He was there

on a visit.

Mrs Gaskitt got

Gus and Gloria up,

gave *them* their breakfasts

and sent them off to school.

She read the paper,

drank a cup of tea,

picked up the post

as it came tumbling

through the letterbox,

opened the door ...

and kissed the

postman!

But what about *Mr* Gaskitt?

Never mind –

he *was* the postman.

It was his latest job.

Meanwhile, Gus and Gloria were in the playground watching – Oh no! – their poor teacher, Mrs Fritter, falling off her bike at the school gates.

Mrs Fritter hit the pavement
with a terrible bang,
got some nasty cuts and bruises
on her arms and legs, and had to go home.

Back in the kitchen,
Mrs Gaskitt was opening the post.
There was a gas bill
and a phone bill
and a postcard from
Grandma Gaskitt on holiday in Spain.

There was a vet's appointment for Horace …

and one more envelope.

Mrs Gaskitt opened it.

Congratulations, Mrs Gaskitt!

said the letter.

You have won first prize in our

most amazing competition.

"Wow!" cried Mrs Gaskitt.

"This must be my lucky day."

Chapter 2
One Little Question

Half an hour later, a van stopped outside the Gaskitts' house. It had Mrs Gaskitt's prize in it: A YEAR'S SUPPLY OF CRUNCHY MICE.

"All I did was answer one little question," said Mrs Gaskitt.

"Fancy that," said the van man.

"And make up one little caption."

"This must be your lucky day," the van man said.

Mrs Gaskitt's prize filled the kitchen.

Horace's friend was amazed.

So was the doormat.

So was Horace.

This must be

my lucky day,

he thought.

CRUNCHY MICE
CRUNCHY MICE
CRUNCHY MICE
CRUNCHY MICE
CRUNCHY MICE
CRUNCHY MICE
CRUNCHY MICE
CRUNCHY MICE
CRUNCHY MICE
CRUNCHY MICE
CRUNCHY MICE
CRUNCHY MICE

Back at the school, a supply teacher

had arrived in Gus and Gloria's classroom.

This supply teacher was

rather short

and rather wide.

She had silvery hair,

dangly earrings,

a big smile …

"Hello, dearies!"

… and a huge suitcase.

On wheels.

"My name," she said, "is Mrs Plum."

And she *opened the case.*

Meanwhile, back in the kitchen,

Horace and his friend were purring loudly and gazing

up at the piles and piles

of Crunchy Mice.

The word had spread.

Horace's other friends were

at the window, peeping in.

"I bet that lot would

last me … a year!"

cried Horace.

"Well, it would," said his friend.

"It's a year's supply."

"Oh, yeah," said Horace.

"Or half a year's supply

for two cats," said his friend.

"Yeah," said Horace.

"Or a month's supply

for twelve cats."

"Yeah!"

"Or a day's supply

for three hundred and sixty-five cats!"

"YEAH!"

"Or a *party,*" miaowed Horace's friends

from outside. "For us."

Chapter 3
Mrs Plum's Suitcase

Mrs Plum took out of her suitcase:

a ball of wool and some knitting

a photograph in a silver frame

a vase of flowers (plastic)

a small guitar

a sandwich maker

a pair of pink fluffy slippers

and a box of

chocolates.

There was silence in the room.

The children gazed in wonder

at Mrs Plum,

the knitting,

the sandwich maker

and the chocolates.

This must be *our* lucky

day, they thought.

Mrs Plum put the flowers

and the photograph on

her desk,

and the slippers on her feet.

She opened the box of chocolates

and popped one into her mouth.

 "Now then, dearies, let's get started."

The day went by in Mrs Plum's class and the children loved it. They had cooking lessons with the sandwich maker, science lessons *fixing* the sandwich maker and singing lessons with the guitar.

Mrs Plum read stories to them, gave them some easy sums and shared her chocolates. When the box was empty, she opened her suitcase and took out another.

By the end of the day

the children could not believe their luck.

Mrs Plum was the best teacher they had ever had.

The best in the school,

in the town,

in the universe!

Yes, everything was perfect.

Well, *almost* everything.

The only trouble was

that in all the excitement

a few little things …

had gone missing.

Billy Turpin had lost his football boots.

Tracey Appledrop had lost her pencil case.

Gloria Gaskitt had lost her lucky charm bracelet.

But even then Mrs Plum

was *so* kind

so helpful

so sympathetic.

She looked everywhere

in that classroom,

searched high and low,

but with no luck at all.

When home-time came,

the missing things were still missing.

Chapter 4
Mrs Gaskitt's Luck Continues

Two days later, Mrs Gaskitt got up again.

Of course, she got up on the day in between

as well, but nothing happened then.

Yes …

Mrs Gaskitt got up,

fed the children,

fed the cats,

read the paper,

drank the tea,

heard a familiar sound

out in the street

– Clink, clink! –

opened the door,

picked up the milk …

and kissed the milkman!

But what about Mr Gaskitt?

Never mind –

he *was* the milkman.

It was his very latest job.

Meanwhile – Oh no! – poor Mrs Fritter

was falling over in the doctor's waiting room.

The doctor had just said

she was well enough to return to work.

Now Mrs Fritter had more cuts and bruises

and needed to go back to bed again.

Meanwhile, Mrs Plum was fit and well.

She played football with the boys,

and netball with the girls.

At playtime, Mrs Plum

drank tea in the staffroom

with the other teachers.

The other teachers liked Mrs Plum.

She told them funny stories

about her long life as a teacher,

shared her chocolates,

and helped them to look for things …

… when they

went missing.

Back at the Gaskitts' house,

the phone was ringing.

Mrs Gaskitt was outside washing her taxi.

In she ran and picked up the receiver.

"Congratulations, Mrs Gaskitt!"

said a man on the phone.

"You have won first prize in our—"

"Wow!" cried Mrs Gaskitt.

"*Another* lucky day."

Chapter 5

One Little Coupon

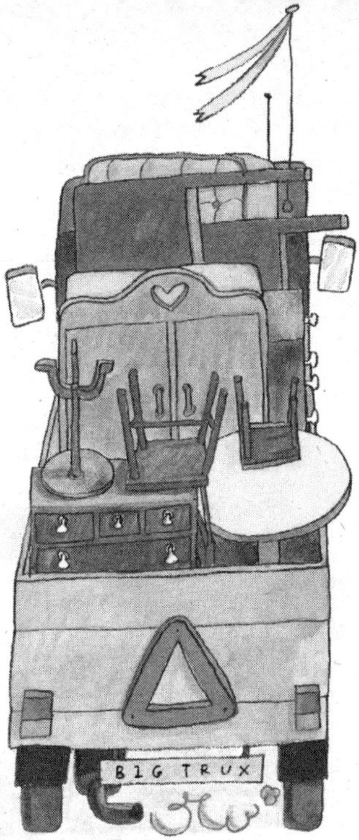

Two hours later, a lorry

"BEEP, BEEP, I AM REVERSING!"

stopped outside the Gaskitts'

house. It had Mrs Gaskitt's

prize in it:

A COMPLETE HOUSEFUL OF FURNITURE!

"All I did was fill in one little coupon,"

said Mrs Gaskitt.

"Well, I never," said the driver.

"And put some ticks in boxes."

"BEEP, BEEP, I AM AMAZED!"

Mrs Gaskitt's prize filled every room in the house (and the kitchen twice over).

Horace and his friend went round sitting on things.

They were amazed too.

"She's very lucky, my Mrs," said Horace.

"I wonder why."

"Perhaps she's got a lucky horseshoe," said his friend. "Or a rabbit's foot – or a four-leaf clover."

"Or a ten-leaf clover," said Horace.

"There's no such thing," said his friend.

"Yes, there is."

"No, there isn't."

"Yes, there is."

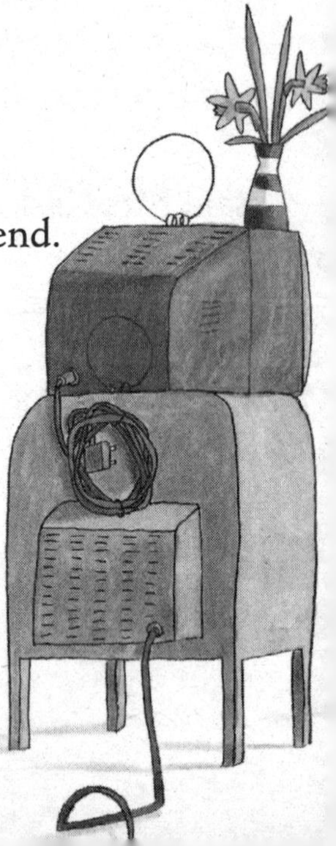

Yes, there is.

Meanwhile, back at the school,

it was almost home-time.

Some of the children had their coats on,

some were lined up by the door

and some …

… were looking for things.

Gus and Gloria were giving Randolph, the class rat,

some clean water and a slice of carrot.

"Now then, dearies," said Mrs Plum.

"Before you go – a message.

I'm planning a little trip soon—"

"Hooray!"

"Great, Miss!"

"I love a trip!"

"Where to, Miss?"

"Where we going?"

"Er … somewhere nice," said Mrs Plum.

"A sort of mystery tour."

"Brilliant!"

"A mystery tour!"

"I love a mystery tour!"

"I've been on one before!"

"I've been on two!"

"Bring £10," Mrs Plum said.

"Tomorrow, if you can."

"I can bring £10, Miss!"

"I can bring twenty!"

"A hundred!"

As the children hurried off,

Mrs Plum called after them.

"One last thing – make it *cash*, dearies."

She popped a chocolate into

Billy Turpin's mouth.

"No cheques."

Chapter 6
Two Thousand Pounds!

The next day Mrs Gaskitt won:

a holiday for four

a caravan

a free hairdo

and a packet

of Protts!!

She told her family

and her friends

and her cat all about it.

"All I did was..."

Horace was pleased, of course,

and proud of Mrs Gaskitt.

But he was puzzled too.

"A holiday for *four* – what use is that?

Should be a holiday for five."

"Or six," said his friend.

"Or eleven," said his other friends

outside the window.

Meanwhile, Mrs Plum had collected

twenty-seven £10 notes from

the children and put them

in a safe place.

On wheels.

The children were excited about the trip,

and excited also about the school fete,

only a day away.

Mr Blagg, the headmaster, made a

little speech about it to the whole school.

There would be book stalls and cake stalls,

raffles and hoop-las, a coconut-shy and

a fancy dress competition.

There'd be a pet show (with prizes),

maypole dancing,

five-a-side for the dads

and an egg-and-spoon race

for the mums.

"Last year, children – Sh!" said Mr Blagg,

"– we raised £1,943.78p for the school fund."

"Hooray!" the children yelled.

"Sh!" said Mr Blagg.

"So this time, let's break the record.

Let's make it – Sh!

– two thousand pounds!"

"Hooray! Hooray!" the children yelled again.

SUMMER FETE
Last year = £1,943.78p
This year
£2,000

Just then, up jumped Mrs Plum.

She couldn't stop herself.

"Two thousand pounds!" she cried,

and her big smile filled the hall.

"I'll help!"

Chapter 7
Some Funny Business

At lunchtime, Mrs Gaskitt

ate her free packet of Protts

and had her free hairdo.

Lucky Mrs Gaskitt.

Meanwhile – Oh no!

– *un*lucky Mrs Fritter.

Mrs Fritter had just popped

into the chemist's for some

painkillers and a bandage.

On her way home and outside the *Travel Agent's*,

she was knocked flying by a short, wide lady

with charming manners,

"Beg pardon, dearie!"

and a huge suitcase.

On wheels.

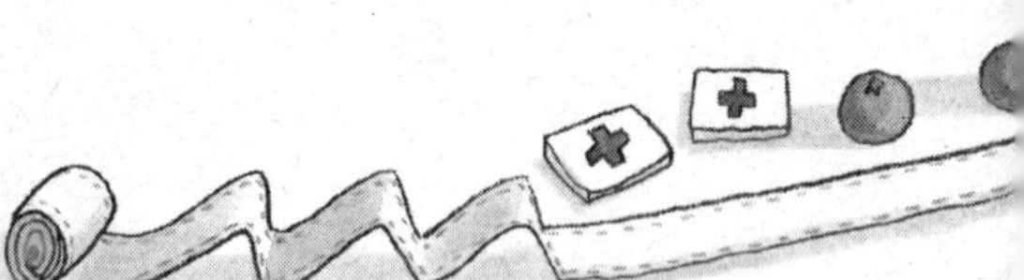

The lady, however,

was very apologetic and *very* kind.

She helped Mrs Fritter to her feet

and gave her a chocolate.

Later that afternoon,

Gus and Billy Turpin were in the classroom

giving Randolph some exercise.

Gloria and Tracey Appledrop were painting a sign

for the Guess the Weight of the Cake competition.

Just then a phone rang.

"A phone, Miss! A phone!"

"Who's ringing us?"

"Where is it?"

Well, would you believe it, the phone was ringing from *inside* Mrs Plum's suitcase.

"It's playing a tune, Miss!"

"So it is, dearie," said Mrs Plum, and she gave the suitcase a kick.

"I know that tune, Miss!"

"Me too!"

"It's the same as Mr Blagg's phone!"

"Yeah!"

"Only he's *lost* his!"

"So he has, dearie," said Mrs Plum and she gave the case another kick.

"I helped him look for it."

Meanwhile, Gus and Gloria and some of the other children were exchanging glances. There was some funny business here. Why did Mrs Plum not open the case? Come to think of it, why did she *never* open it (apart from that first morning)?

All of a sudden,

the whole class became suspicious.

They smelled a rat, all right …

and it was *not* Randolph.

Chapter 8
Handsome Horace

The next day,

which was a Saturday,

Mrs Gaskitt leapt out of bed,

raced downstairs,

flew into the

crowded kitchen:

2 tables

8 chairs

25 cartons of Crunchy Mice,

CRUNCHY MICE
CRUNCHY MICE
CRUNCHY MICE
CRUNCHY MICE
CRUNCHY MICE
CRUNCHY MICE
CRUNCHY MICE

fed the children,

fed Horace,

read the paper,

read the post,

opened the back door,

kissed the milkman …

… and went red in the face.

It was the wrong milkman.

Meanwhile, Gus and Gloria

were grooming Horace.

They brushed his coat till it shone,

tied a new pink ribbon around his neck

and told him how handsome he was.

Horace purred with pride.

He wished his friend was there to see him.

Later that morning,

Mrs Gaskitt was

still rushing around –

finding her trainers,

boiling an egg –

while Gus and Gloria

followed her about and

tried to get her attention.

"It's that supply teacher, Mum."

"Hm." Mrs Gaskitt was cooling her egg.

"The one with the suitcase."

"Yes." Mrs Gaskitt was

putting her trainers on.

"Which she *never* opens!"

"Ah." Mrs Gaskitt was

getting a spoon from

the cutlery drawer.

"Well, *we* think ..."

Mrs Gaskitt was out

through the door,

"... she's definitely ..."

into the garden

and off down the path

with her egg and spoon.

"... up to something!"

Chapter 9
Mrs Plum Lends a Hand

It was a warm May afternoon.

The school fete was in full swing.

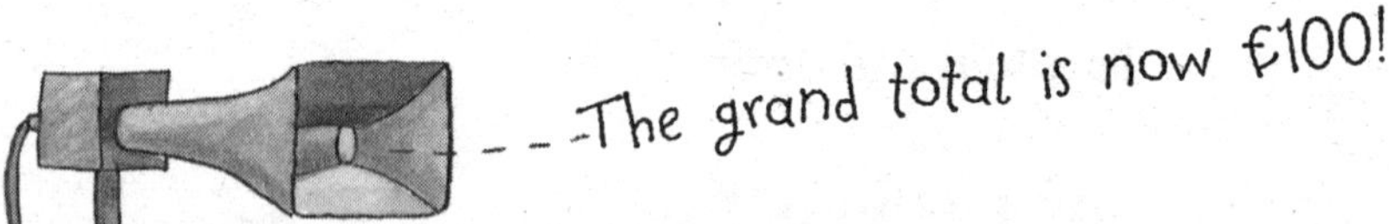

The maypole dancers were dancing

and delicious smells:

ice-cream

candy-floss

hot dogs

filled the air.

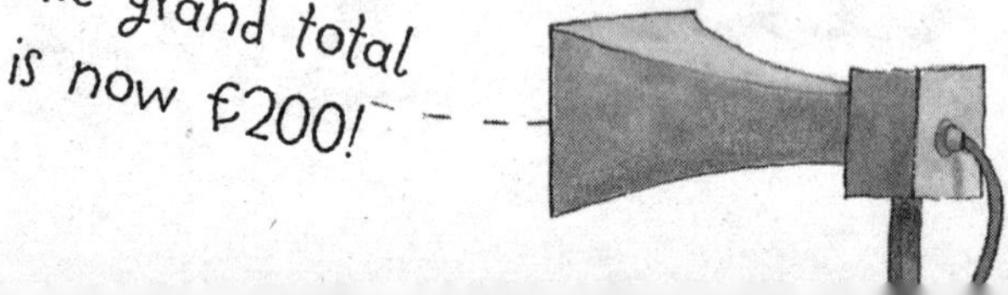

Mums and dads were working hard.

The infants were rushing

around in their

fancy dress

costumes.

Horace, with his beautiful ribbon,

was lined up with the other pets

in the pet show.

And the money …

… was

pouring

in.

Meanwhile, Mrs Gaskitt was winning things.

She guessed the weight of the cake,

"All I did was..."

and the number of sweets in a jar.

She won a teddy,

a bottle of wine,

three goldfish,

five kilograms of grass seed

and a lawnmower.

And Horace saw … most of it.

He purred with pride.

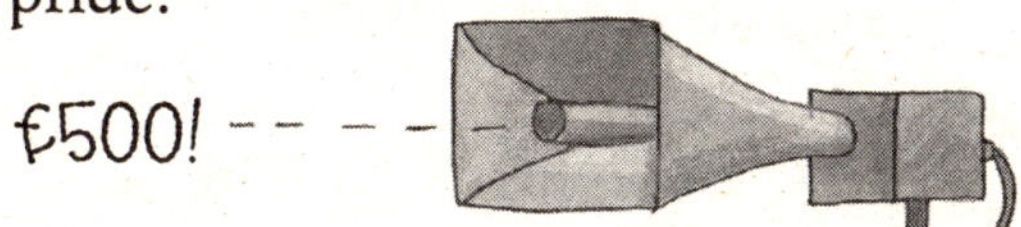

"I know her," he told a guinea pig.

"Oh yes." The guinea pig was not interested in Mrs Gaskitt.

He had other worries.

"Do I look stupid in this bow?"

"No," said Horace. "Not really."

The guinea pig scowled. "Hm. Bet I do."

But, of course, what (you will be

wanting to know),

what about Mrs Plum?

Well, Mrs Plum was here,

there and everywhere.

She helped with

the refreshments.

She helped with the fancy dress.

She helped with the coconut shy.

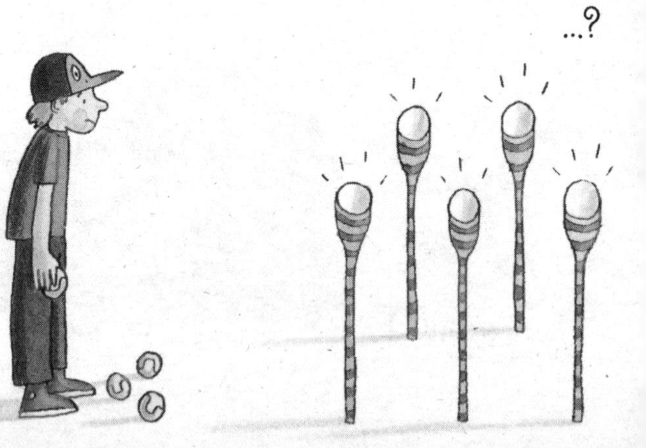

The children – Gus and Gloria,

Tracey, Billy and the others – followed

Mrs Plum and watched her like hawks.

But the crowds were so big, the noise so loud,

the delicious smells so … delicious,

that the children didn't *always* see

what she was up to.

Meanwhile, Mr Blagg …

was looking happier,

and happier,

and happier.

Horace's new friend was looking happier too.

He had just won a rosette.

"So what's your name then?" he asked.

"Horace," said Horace.

"Fancy that – mine's Maurice. Horace and Maurice!"

"Yeah," said Horace, "all we need is a Boris."

"Or a Doris," said Maurice.

"Or a … Poris," said Horace.

"*Poris?* There's no such name."

"Yes, there is," said Horace.

"No, there isn't."

Now, Mrs Gaskitt

and the other mothers were lining up …

... for the egg-and-spoon race.

Mr Blagg

jumped on his chair.

"We've made it –

Sh!" he yelled.

"Grand total –

two thousand

pounds!"

"Hooray!" "Hooray!"

The crowd cheered, then cheered again

as the egg-and-spoon race began.

It was a tremendous contest.

First Mrs Turpin was in the lead,

then she dropped her egg.

Then Mrs Appledrop was in the lead

and she dropped her egg.

Then Mrs Gaskitt

was in the lead and...

Meanwhile, all eyes (except two)

were on the race.

The children were watching (and yelling).

Horace was watching (and purring with pride).

Even Mr Blagg on his chair

was watching.

All of a sudden, Mr Blagg

looked down at the table and

was *not* happy any more.

The cash box,

the two thousand pounds,

even Mr Blagg's favourite pencil

(which his dear old mother

had given him) …

had disappeared.

Chapter 10
Oops!

Now, of course, there was uproar at the school fete. Everyone was yelling and rushing around.

Well, nearly everyone.

Meanwhile, the egg-and-spoon race was still in progress.

Mrs Gaskitt got up speed, while her egg, luckily, stayed on its spoon. She ran like the wind, broke the tape, won the race, and –

Oh no! – *collided* with a short, wide lady,

silvery hair,

big smile,

suitcase (on wheels)

and knocked her flying.

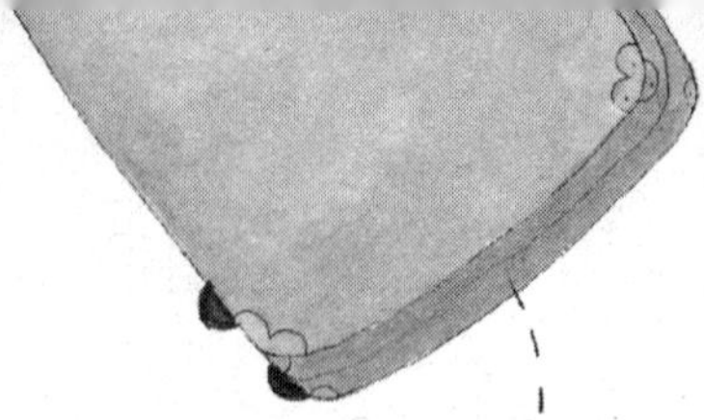

Knocked her

suitcase flying too,

which rolled

and bounced

and rolled again …

and burst open.

The crowd was astonished…

And all that Mrs Plum,

as she sat on the grass

with an egg in her lap,

could think to say was…

Later, when the police arrived,

Mrs Plum had rather

more to say.

"Can't think what came

over me, dearies."

She smiled at Mr Blagg.

"Never done anything like this before."

"Yes, you have," said the inspector. "Loads of times."

"She's a very clever woman," the inspector explained.

"Thank you, dearie!"

"Robbed more schools than I've had hot dinners. Been on her trail for ages."

The inspector shook hands with Mr Blagg and congratulated Mrs Gaskitt on her lucky collision.

"This should put a stop to Mrs Plum

(alias Mrs Peach, alias Mrs Pomegranate)

and her little games for a while,

I shouldn't wonder."

He climbed into his

police car.

Chapter 11
Mrs Gaskitt's Luck Runs Out

It was a warm May evening.

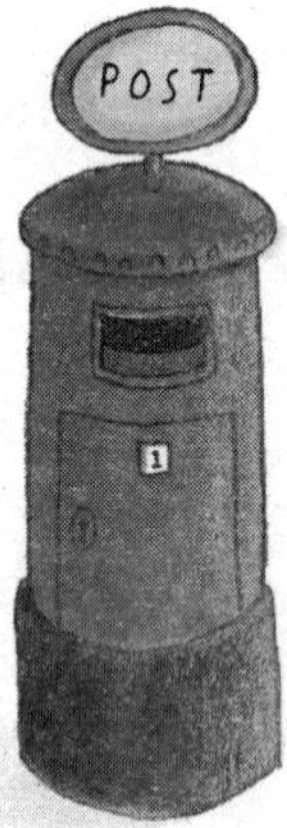

Mrs Gaskitt walked home

with her children,

her cat and her prizes.

Gus and Gloria were telling

their mum all about Mrs Plum.

Mrs Gaskitt was telling

Gus and Gloria

(and Horace)

how she had won

the teddy,

the bottle of wine

and all the other things.

"All I did..."

Suddenly, not looking

where she was going,

Mrs Gaskitt walked

straight under a

window cleaner's ladder.

Oh no! – *un*lucky Mrs Gaskitt.

Water from the window

cleaner's bucket

came splashing down and

soaked her to the skin.

And that wasn't the end of it.

Next thing, would you believe it,

the *window cleaner himself*

came scrambling down,

grabbed Mrs Gaskitt,

hauled her to her feet –

– and kissed her!

But what about *Mr* Gaskitt?

Well, you've guessed it,

haven't you?

Yes – it was

his latest job.

Meanwhile, Horace was thinking hard ...

about luck.

Hm. Lucky rabbit's foot – no.

Lucky horseshoes – no.

Lucky four-leaf clovers – no.

Lucky black cats...

It was a warm May night.

The Gaskitts were asleep

in their crowded bedrooms.

The goldfish were getting

used to their new home.

The garage was full of grass seed.

Horace and his friend were

downstairs playing cards.

"It's you!" said Horace.

"What is?" said his friend. "SNAP! – I win."

"That's it – you always win!" said Horace.

"You're the *lucky black cat!*"

"No, I'm not – SNAP!" said his friend.

"Yes, you are."

"No, I'm not."

"Yes, you are."

"No, I'm not."

"Yes, you are."

"No, I'm … not!"

"Yes … you … *yawn* … are."

CRUNCHY MICE
That's ALL FOLKS!
THE END

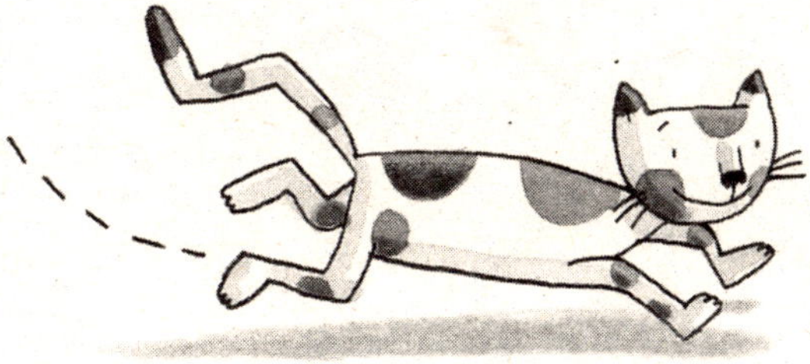

Once More...

The Gaskitts!

The Cat Who got Carried away

USEFUL MAPS

Contents

IN THIS GRAND AND GRIPPING

Mr Gaskitt

spends most of

his time hoovering.

Gus and Gloria

have a lot of running to do.

Gaskitts Story

Mrs Gaskitt

hardly ever gets

out of bed.

And Horace –

poor Horace! – ends up ...

in a pet shop!

★★★ **Also Starring** ★★★

A rat named **Randolph,**

a guinea pig named **Maurice**

and a teacher named **Mrs Fritter**

(who sometimes falls over).

Not to mention a mysterious

gang of... But more of them later.

ON WITH THE STORY!

Chapter 1
The Barking Pram

Early one evening the Gaskitts were at home

sitting side by side on Mr and Mrs Gaskitt's bed.

All except Mrs Gaskitt – she was in bed.

Why is that?

It's only half past seven.

Anyway, there they were

drinking tea,

eating biscuits

and looking at the

family photo album.

There was a photo of Gus and Gloria as babies, a photo of Horace as a kitten and a photo of Mr and Mrs Gaskitt … dancing.

"On our honeymoon," said Mr Gaskitt.

"But what about us?"

"Were we born then?"

the children cried.

"Not quite," said Mrs Gaskitt.

"We had the house to ourselves."

"Yes." Mr Gaskitt smiled.

"It was delightful."

(Gloria punched him.)

"I mean boring."

(And Gus hit him

with a pillow.)

Meanwhile, Horace was outside

sitting on the garden wall

watching the world go by.

He saw a boy on a bike,

a boy on a skateboard,

a woman in a car

and, finally,

on the other side of the road,

a man absolutely *whizzing* along

with a really old pram.

And the strange thing was,

which Horace noticed,

the strange thing was, the pram …

was barking.

Chapter 2
Fried Egg and Pineapple

The next morning

everybody got up.

Gus and Gloria got up

and went to school.

Mr Gaskitt got up

and went shopping.

Mrs Gaskitt got up, got the paper,

got the post,

got a cup of tea

and a *cream doughnut* ...

and went back to bed.

Meanwhile, Horace was out on the wall again

hoping to see and hear that

mysterious pram.

Well, Horace never saw
the pram that time,
but Mr Gaskitt did.

He was in his car at the school crossing
and there it was, the same as before,
with the same man just *whizzing* along.
But not barking, though. Oh, no!
It was more like … squeaking,
Mr Gaskitt thought.

When Gus and Gloria got to school

they found that something

dreadful had happened.

Randolph – clever, lovable Randolph –

the class rat, had ("Squeak, squeak!") ...

disappeared.

Oh yes, and Mrs Fritter,

while trying to find him,

had fallen out of a window.

The children, of course,

were terribly upset.

"Poor Randolph!" they cried.

"Poor Randolph!"

"Poor Randolph!"

Oh yes,

and poor

Mrs Fritter.

By this time Mr Gaskitt was in the supermarket filling his trolley.

Horace was visiting a friend who *seemed* to be out.

Mrs Gaskitt was also out …

of bed.

She was downstairs now in the sitting-room watching TV, with a mug of hot chocolate and a fried egg and pineapple –

– yes, pineapple sandwich.

Meanwhile, somewhere not very far away, that pram was …

... still whizzing along.

So, let's follow the pram, shall we? Here's a useful map. It shows where the pram has been so far this morning and where it's going.

Hm ... and here's a big white van with a ramp. Now the pram is being pushed into the van.

Ha-ha!

What's going on here?

And look!

There's Horace on a wall again, outside his friend's house.

Horace is a smart cat. Well, *Horace* thinks he is. He's thinking now that if he sits here for a while, his friend will show up … or something *interesting* might happen.

It probably will.

Chapter 3
Meet Mr Cruncher

Back at school Gus and Gloria

and the other children

were in the classroom

whispering about Randolph –

"Poor Randolph!"

"Poor Randolph!"

– and waiting for the

supply teacher. (Mrs Fritter

– nasty cuts and bruises –

had gone home in a taxi.)

Suddenly – Bang! –

the classroom

door flew open,

the windows rattled,

the floor shook …

and there he was.

Very tall.

Very wide.

With a great big

heavy bag.

And his name was

MR CRUNCHER!

Mr Cruncher was

a PE teacher,

a keep-fit fiend.

He had been in the army.

He had been in the navy.

He was a man of few

words … and he *loved*

running.

Mr Blagg, the headmaster,

shook hands with

Mr Cruncher –

– and wished he hadn't.

Mr Cruncher said, "Good morning, class!"

and the windows rattled again.

After that the lessons began.

During the morning

Mr Cruncher taught

reading, writing

and *running*.

But mostly running.

There were obstacle races

in the classroom, relay races

in the hall and laps and laps

... on the school field.

By lunchtime

Gus and Gloria

and the others

had forgotten

Randolph,

and were puffing

and gasping

and sleeping even

... on the grass.

Meanwhile,

where's Horace?

He was on that wall

when we last saw him,

wasn't he?

But he's not there now.

Meanwhile also,

where's the pram?

Well, it's still

whizzing along – look!

Down the road,

round the corner,

up the ramp …

and into the van.

It seems a bit odd,

that pram, doesn't it?

Let's take a closer look.

Let's see what

sort of *baby*

it's got in there.

Let's see, closer,

closer,

and closer...

Oh, no –

– they've got

Horace!

Chapter 4
Have You Seen This Hamster?

By two o'clock that afternoon

trouble was brewing all over town.

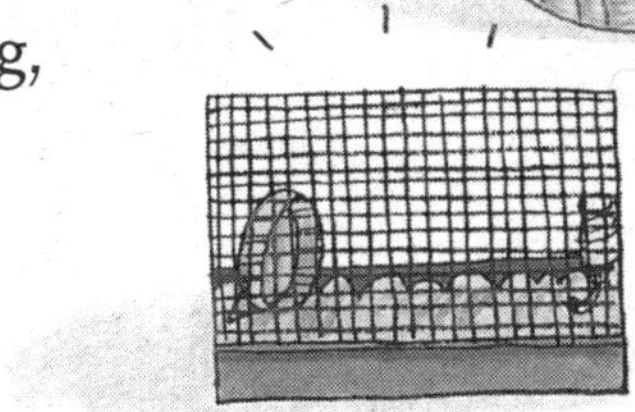

There were cats missing,

and dogs missing,

gerbils,

guinea pigs – even goldfish!

Even budgerigars!

Even – well,

not just at this moment,

but fairly soon now – even *penguins!*

Yes, sad owners wandered

up and down the streets

whistling and calling,

"Here, Tibby!"

"Here, Marmaduke!"

"Here, Sweetie Pie!"

Some of them

put posters up,

HAVE YOU SEEN

THIS HAMSTER?

Some phoned

for the police.

Back at the school

the children heard

none of this.

All they knew about

was Randolph.

"Poor Randolph!"

All they cared about was

their sore feet.

For the literacy hour

Mr Cruncher had them

lifting heavy books.

In science

he had them

lifting …

each other!

And for music and art

and home economics

… he had them running.

When they got home,

Gus and Gloria sat on

their mother's bed

and told her

all about it.

"It's dreadful,

Mum!"

"Our legs are

dropping off!"

"We're worn out!"

"Dear me," said Mrs Gaskitt,

or rather, "Drr … mrr…"

She was eating a sandwich

at the time.

Yes, fried egg and

pineapple again.

Also, as you can see,

she was *in* bed again.

And it isn't even teatime.

Meanwhile, downstairs, Mr Gaskitt was cooking the children's tea, doing a bit of ironing and listening to the radio.

"THE MYSTERY OF THE MISSING PETS!"

yelled the radio.

"CATS AND DOGS VANISHING INTO THIN AIR!"

"POLICE BAFFLED!"

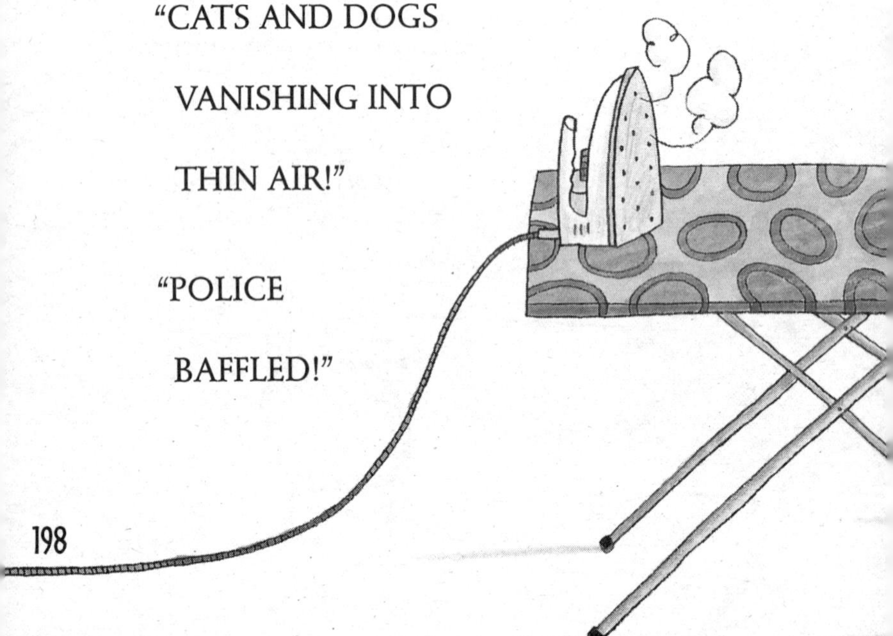

Mr Gaskitt folded a shirt
and put it on a pile.
He looked in the oven,
peered out of the
window and opened
the kitchen door.
"Hm." Mr Gaskitt gazed
thoughtfully into the garden
and rubbed his chin.

"Where's
Horace?"

So where *is* Horace?

Time, perhaps, for another useful map.

This one shows where the van went with Horace in it. Ha-ha!

Looks like they've taken him to the next town!

It also shows (it's a *very* useful map) where the Number 9 bus goes.

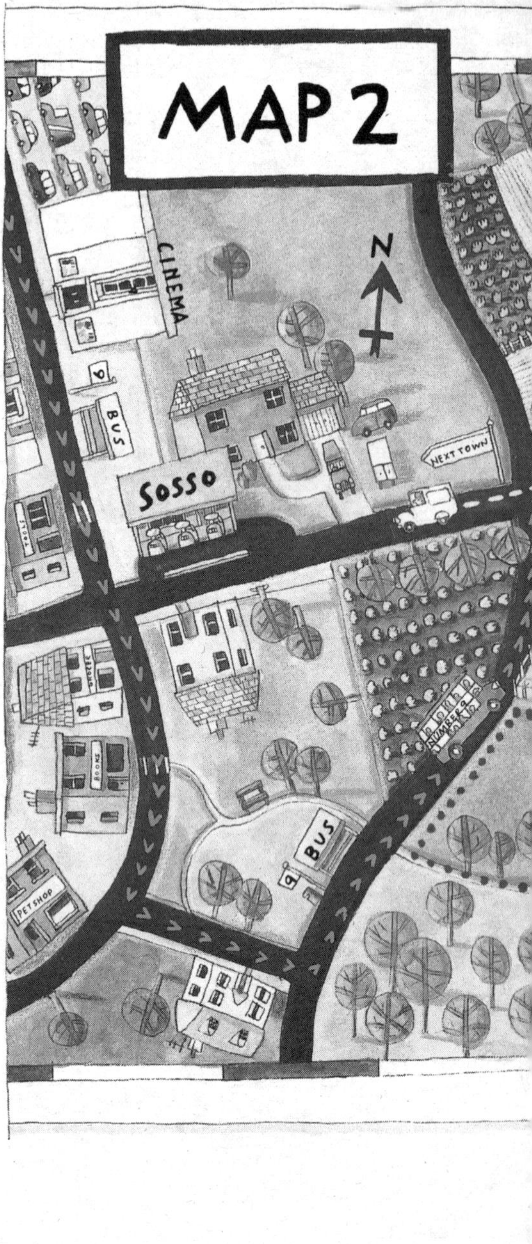

That could come

in handy.

And where,

tomorrow morning

bright and early –

actually, it's

going to rain –

Gus and Gloria

and the others

may very well,

if Mr Cruncher

gets his way,

may very well …

be *running*.

Chapter 5
Honest Joe

That night Gus and Gloria did not sleep a wink.

All they could think about was,

They had walked the streets

and knocked on doors

and looked *everywhere* …

but couldn't find him.

Mr and Mrs Gaskitt

– look, she's out of bed! –

had driven all round the town

and *they* couldn't find him.

Meanwhile, in the *next* town ...

in the back room of a pet shop

a large number of unhappy pets

were barking

and squealing

and twittering

and so on,

hoping to be let out.

Upstairs above the shop Honest Joe was

playing cards with his

honest mother and his

honest Uncle Sid.

Pet shop? *Pet* shop?

What's going on here?

And who's "Honest Joe"?

Well, Honest Joe –

it's time now you were told –

thinks of himself as a sort of *pet collector*.

He rescues animals, or so he says,

that are lost or strayed

and finds them nice

new cosy homes.

His mother and his uncle

help him in this work.

Usually they travel

round from town to town,

open a little shop for a while,

make a little money,

play a little cards …

and travel on.

Honest Joe means no harm.

He would not hurt a fly

– or so he says –

or a gerbil …

or a cat.

The worst he'd ever do

is put them in a shop –

Oh no, poor Horace! –

and sell them.

Chapter 6
The Great Escape

It was half past six in the morning.

Horace Gaskitt sat in the window

of Honest Joe's Pet Shop,

watching the world go by.

Horace was a brainy cat.

Well, Horace thought he was.

He was thinking now,

and had been thinking

since Honest Uncle Sid had grabbed him,

he was thinking now … how to escape.

Meanwhile, in the window next to

Horace – sat Randolph!

He was thinking of escaping too.

"What we need is a plan," said Horace.

"We could dig a tunnel, maybe –

or get a glass-cutter!"

Hm. Randolph said nothing,

but rubbed his little chin.

Randolph, you see, really *was* brainy.

He lived in a school after all.

Randolph was educated.

Horace now was getting carried away.

"It could be great!" he cried. "Like that movie –

The Great Escape!

We could be famous –

on TV – wow!"

And he said (or rather yelled),

"We could make a rope ladder!

We could disguise ourselves!"

"No," said Randolph.

He was studying the

wire pen they were in.

"I've got a better idea.

Wake that guinea pig up."

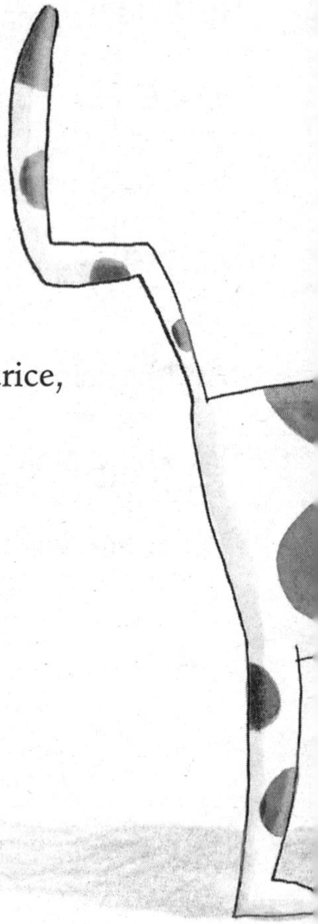

The guinea pig's name was Maurice,

and he was not really asleep,

just fed up.

"It's hopeless," he groaned.

"We'll never get out."

"Yes, we will," said Randolph.

"Climb on Horace's back."

"What for?" said Maurice,

but he did it anyway.

And then – look at that!

Randolph, clever Randolph,

climbs up on Maurice's back

(on his head, actually),

and

stretches

and

stretches

and

stretches up …

to the catch …

on the door …

of the pen.

Chapter 7
That Pram Again

Now the pace is quickening.

Now things are hotting up.

Now ... well, you get the idea.

Anyway, here's the TIMETABLE

6:45

Horace, Maurice and Randolph tiptoe – Sh! – out of the shop window.

7:30

Honest Joe, Mrs Gaskitt, Mrs Fritter and Mr Cruncher have their breakfasts. In different places, of course.

8:15

Honest Joe's mother loads the pram into the van and drives off with Honest Uncle Sid.

At the same time, Horace, Maurice and Randolph creep out through the open door and run off down the street.

8:55

Gus and Gloria and the others get changed for their cross-country run.

The rain begins to fall. Five minutes later, Mrs Fritter falls too,

tripping up over a rug on her way to the bathroom.

9:15

Uncle Sid takes his "baby" for a stroll in the *zoo*.

The Number 9 bus, meanwhile, leaves Fish Street – eight minutes late.

9:30

Mrs Gaskitt sits up in bed. She has a funny look on her face. Can you see? She looks happy and sad at the same time.

9:45

Mr Cruncher and his class are off – "Puff, gasp!" – on their run.

At the same time, down a little street at the back of the zoo – look, here it comes! – that pram again, with Honest Uncle Sid

... just *whizzing* along.

Chapter 8
Clever Randolph!

Horace, Maurice and Randolph

were hiding behind a litter bin

next to a bus shelter.

Randolph was thoughtful.

Maurice was gloomy.

And Horace …

was getting carried away.

"It's like in that movie!" he cried.

"*The Incredible Journey* – where these pets

travel thousands and thousands of miles

to get back home!"

"Was one of them a guinea pig?" said Maurice.

"Can't remember," said Horace.

"Anyway, we could do that! Hide out in a barn – follow the stars at night … have adventures."

But Randolph only coughed and rubbed his little chin.

"No," he said. "I've got a better idea."

Meanwhile, outside the zoo,

Honest Uncle Sid was whizzing along

with a pramful of penguins.

Yes – penguins!

He was supposed to get *parrots*

but Uncle Sid had always

wanted a penguin.

Or two.

Or eight.

Anyway, there he was,

whizzing along,

when who should

he spy outside the scout hut

but a little tiny tied-up spotted dozy … dog.

"Room for one more!"

cried Uncle Sid.

And he grabbed up the little dog and was just pushing him in with the penguins, when …

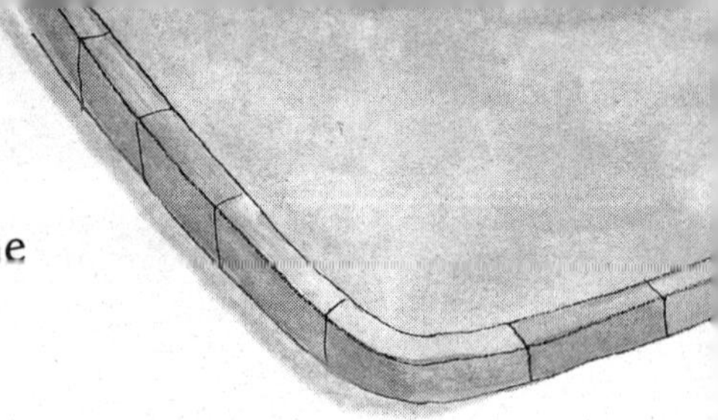

round the corner came

Gus and Gloria and

Tracey and Billy and a few others.

Meanwhile also,

Mr and Mrs Gaskitt were driving by.

They spotted Gus and Gloria and waved …

but couldn't stop. Mr Gaskitt was

taking Mrs Gaskitt – Oh, no! –

to the hospital.

What's wrong?

Is she poorly?

She doesn't look poorly.

Meanwhile *also*, the

Number 9 bus was…

But things are getting

a bit complicated,

don't you think?

Perhaps we

could do with …

one more map.

See – there's the pram with the van parked round the corner.

There's Gus and Gloria and the others, including Mr Cruncher.

There's Mr and Mrs Gaskitt in their car.

There's the Number 9 bus.

And there –

can you see? –

upstairs on the

bus, on the front

seat, side by side,

cosy, safe and

sharing a bag of

crisps they've

found …

there's Horace,

and Maurice

and …

clever

Randolph.

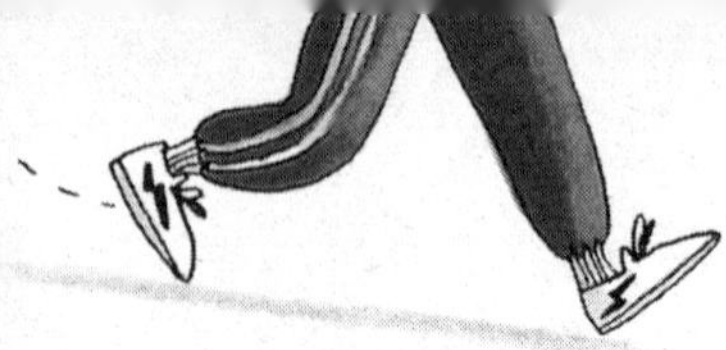

Chapter 9
Running Like the Wind

But what happened *next*, you'll say. Hm … well, let's see.

Uncle Sid whizzed off with his once more barking pram. (That little dozy dog was wide awake now.)

Like a rocket he went, round the corner, down the street, up the ramp, into the van … and away.

And after him

came Gus

and Gloria

and Billy

and Tracey.

And Marigold

and Mary

and Tom

and Rupert

and Buster

and Polly

and Esmeralda

and Mr Cruncher …

and a few others.

So the race

began. The race?

Race? Between

a van and children?

Yes – and it was much

closer than you'd think.

See – the children

were young, strong,

and ran like the wind.

Mr Cruncher was

proud of them.

Meanwhile, the van was old, stolen and

had failed its MOT.

So what with traffic-lights and

zebra crossings and so on, Gus and Gloria

and the others

kept up with it …

down this road,

down that,

up this hill,

over that bridge …

all the way to

the next town.

All the way, in fact, to *Honest Joe's.*

Honest Joe, meanwhile,

was hard at work serving

a customer.

Suddenly in burst

his honest mother,

his honest uncle,

a grumpy little

barking dog,

four or five penguins –

"*Penguins!*" cried Joe.

"Where's the parrots?" –

and a whole

classful of hot

and steaming …

"K I D S !"

Not to mention

Mr Cruncher.

Then the *battle* began.

Well, it wasn't

much of a battle.

Honest Joe's mother

tried to sneak off,

but tripped up over a

penguin and was sat on

by some of the bigger girls.

And the penguin.

Honest

Joe punched

Mr Cruncher in

the tummy –

– and wished

he hadn't.

Honest Uncle Sid

looked at the odds,

shrugged his shoulders

and surrendered.

Meanwhile, at the hospital, Mrs Gaskitt was in bed *again*. A doctor with a stethoscope was listening to *her* tummy. Hm. What's going on here? Let's have a listen too.

Shall we?

Sh…

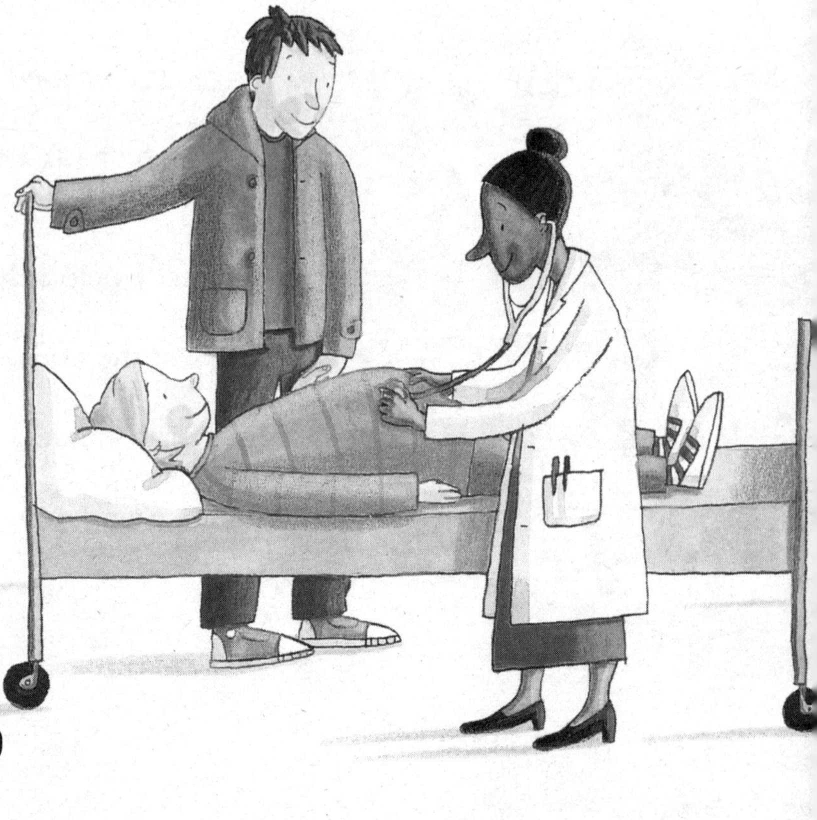

Where am I?

What's happening?

It's very dark in here.

I could just eat a doughnut.

Oh – here we go!

It's getting lighter...

Where? Where...

"Waaaa!"

So there we are. (Did you guess?)

At half past one in the afternoon

on a Wednesday

in September

Mrs Gaskitt (and Mr Gaskitt too)

had – their – baby.

Little Gary Gaskitt:
brown hair
blue eyes
7lb 12oz

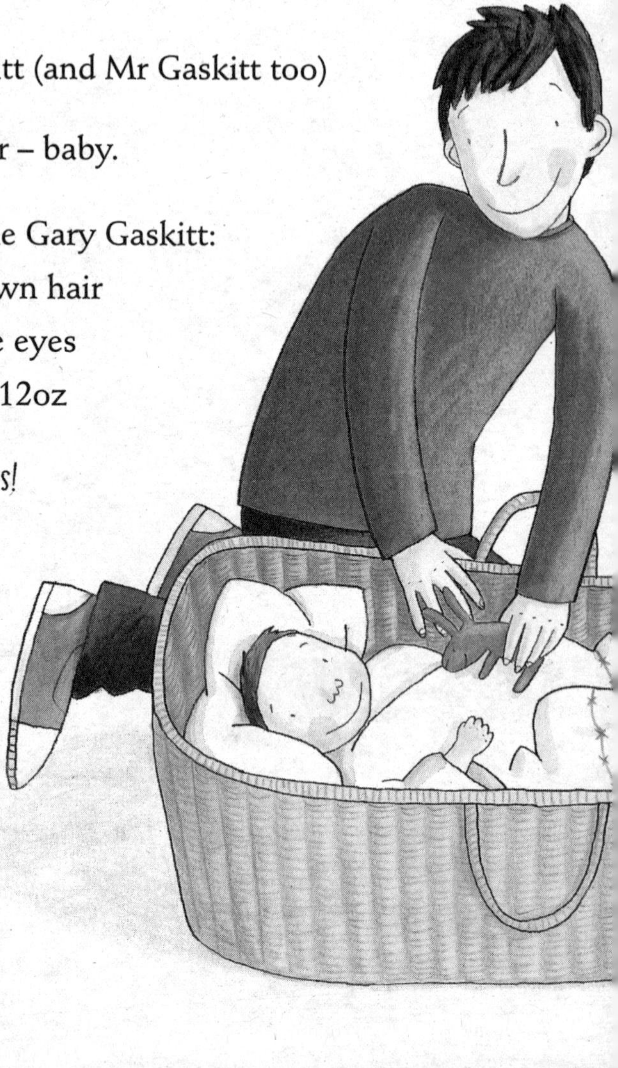

Chapter 10
The Final Timetable

Now the pace is slowing.

Now things are winding down.

Now ... well, you get the idea.

Anyway, here's the final

TIMETABLE

1:30

Little Gary Gaskitt arrives.

1:45

The police arrive (not at the hospital, though) and load Honest Joe and his gang into a van.

The police are happy. They have captured some dangerous criminals – and got their dog back.

2:15

Meanwhile, Gus and Gloria and the other children are sad. All these rescued pets, but where's Horace? Where's Randolph? And where (if they'd only ever heard of him), where's Maurice?

2:40

The children arrive ... back at the school.

There they are!

4:00

In the police cell Honest Joe and his mother play a little cards ...

and win a little money.

5:30

Mrs Fritter watches TV and thinks of going back to school.

Mr Cruncher goes off for an early evening run with his girlfriend.

At the same time, Mr Gaskitt drives Gus and Gloria and Horace to the hospital ... for the happy ending.

Chapter 11
Meanwhile...

One week later the Gaskitts –

all five of them –

were at home sitting

side by side on the sofa.

All except little Gary.

He was in his carrycot.

Anyway,

there they were

drinking coffee,

eating cake and

sticking photos

of Gary in the

family album.

There was a photo of Gary –

aged one hour,

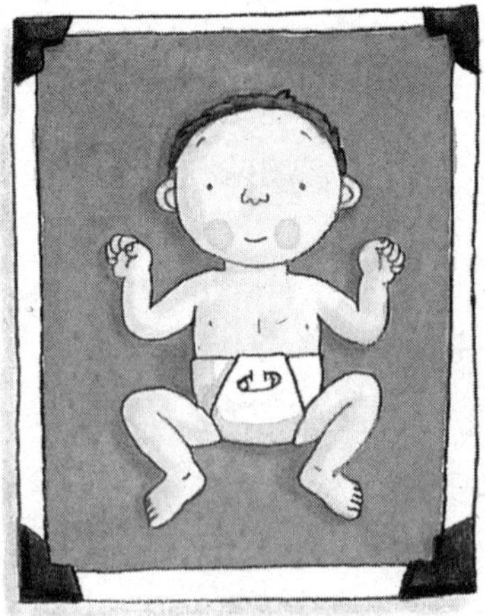

a photo of Gary –

aged one day,

a photo of Gary –

aged two days …

and so on.

Meanwhile, little Gary himself just lies there

in his cot and watches the world go by.

Gary Gaskitt is a clever baby.

(Well, Mrs Gaskitt thinks he is.)

He's thinking now

that if he lies there

long enough, something –

– something

interesting

might happen.

It probably will.

Bye-bye!

The Gaskitts ...

... again!

The Children Who Smelled a Rat

Contents

Meet The Gaskitts

Mr Gaskitt
The dad.

Mrs Gaskitt
The mum
and taxi-driver.

Gary Gaskitt
The baby.
Eyes blue,
hair brown,
weight
~~7lb 12oz~~
~~8lb 4oz~~
9lb 10oz.

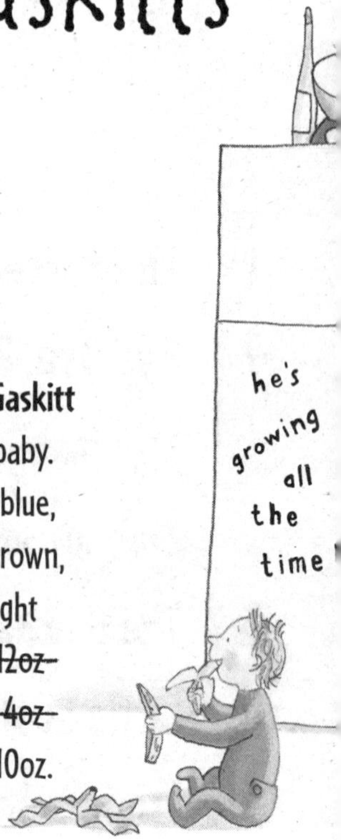

Horace Gaskitt: The cat.
Horace has lots of friends.

Gus and Gloria Gaskitt
The twins.

Picture dictionary
(some useful words and phrases)

*Actually, there's no jelly and ice-cream in this story, but we thought you'd like to see it, all the same.

Chapter 1
The Parcel

One winter's day a forgetful man  in a green  hat and a great  hurry left his  umbrella on a train, his  briefcase in a bookshop, his  book – which he had only just bought – on a park bench, and his very important parcel  in a taxi.

Later on, much later actually, when the man came home again, he left his  hat on his head, forgot his  supper, and went to  bed.*

---

* Which is the last we'll hear of him!

Meanwhile, on that same day, it was a Friday,

Mrs Gaskitt *found* a parcel in her taxi.

And when she picked it up,

the parcel went …

Chapter 2

Bye Bye, Baby

Mr Gaskitt was minding the baby.

It was his turn.

And doing the shopping

and opening the boot

and feeling in his pocket

for the car-park ticket

and tying his shoelace

and whistling a little tune

and *looking the other way.*

Meanwhile, little Gary: eyes blue,

hair brown,

weight 10lb 3oz,

was ...

... rolling away.

Chapter 2 ½: "Tweet, Tweet!"

Horace was at home watching the goldfish when Mrs Gaskitt came in with the parcel, unwrapped it, scratched her head,

had a cup of tea

and went out again.

Horace watched the parcel, and the unwrapping.

It was, of course – you guessed, didn't you? – a little bird in a cage.

A teeny, tiny, little bird lost and all alone …

with a cat.

Chapter 2¾: 10lb 5oz

Meanwhile, little Gary …

was still rolling away.

Chapter 3
The Teacher Who Wasn't Herself

So there we are,
a bad day for a little bird,
a bad day for a little baby,
and a bad day, too,
come to think of it,
for Gus and Gloria.

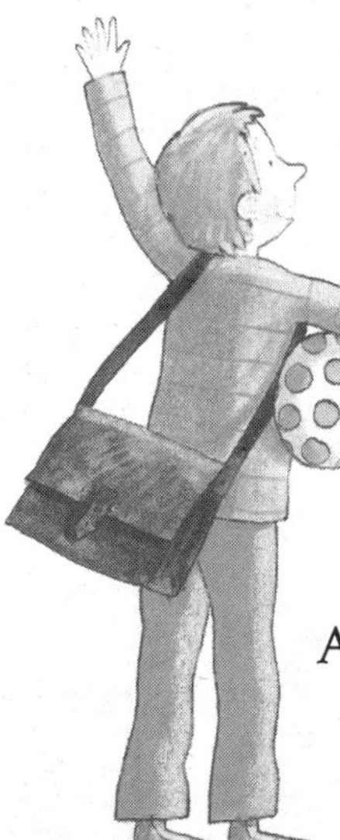

Actually, they had had a bad *week*.

On Monday

their teacher,

Mrs Fritter, fell off

her bike at the school gates

and had to go home.

And the supply

teacher was …

… Mr Blotter.

On Tuesday

Mrs Fritter came back,

tripped over a skipping rop

and went away again.

And the supply

teacher was …

… Mr Cruncher.

On Wednesday and Thursday

Mrs Fritter was

run over by a lady

with a pushchair

and trodden on

in the doctor's

waiting room.

And the supply

teacher was …

… Mrs Doom.

Now it was Friday, and Mrs Fritter, with her arm in a sling, was back again, well, sort of.

But the children were puzzled.

Mrs Fritter had a funny look in her eye.

She seemed to have forgotten

where things were kept,

and – worse still –

ALL THEIR NAMES.

Chapter 4
Little Lost Bird

Horace was back at the house watching the bird.

A bird, he thought. A teeny, tiny, little bird, lost and all alone.

And he thought,

Cats eat birds … hm.

The bird was watching Horace. She fluffed her feathers, flicked her tail, opened her teeny, tiny beak and spoke.

"Come here," said the bird.

"Er … right," said Horace.

"Look into my eyes," said the bird.

"Right," said Horace.

"Do as I say," said the bird.

"Why should I?" said Horace.

"Do as I say!"

"Er … right," said Horace.

Meanwhile, one teeny, tiny baby,

getting bigger though, 10lb 6oz,

was – do you remember? –

still rolling away.

Still in the shopping trolley,

but now on the back of a

lorry – did you see that? –

and being chased

by his dad.

Mr Gaskitt was

running

hard.

Actually, if he'd only known it,

he could have caught a taxi.

Mrs Gaskitt, at that very moment,

was driving by.

But Mrs Gaskitt never saw

him, or the baby.

She was watching the car in

front, sucking a humbug,

thinking of getting her

hair cut, puzzling

over that little bird,

and *looking the*

other way.

Meanwhile, back at the house …

… said the bird.

Chapter 5

Frightening Mrs Fritter

Gus and Gloria's class liked Mrs Fritter.

She was the kindest,

friendliest,

and most popular

teacher in the whole school.

Well, usually.

But today, as you can see and *hear* –

things (and thingies) were different.

Mrs Fritter frightened

everybody.

She frightened Randolph,

the class rat, who hid in his cage,

and Mr Blagg,

the headmaster,

who hid in his office.

When Mr Cruncher

came back

for his dumbbells,

she even frightened him.

The children whispered

and passed little notes

to each other,

and smelled a rat.

Actually, they really did smell a rat.

Mrs Fritter wouldn't let them clean Randolph's cage out. They smelled a couple of gerbils too, and a hamster.

At playtime

Mrs Fritter went to the staffroom

and ...

frightened the teachers.

Mr Blagg sneaked in, grabbed a cup of coffee

and a Kit Kat and sneaked out again.

Back in the classroom Randolph

sneaked out for a bit of biscuit.

Out in the playground

Gus, Gloria and the others

frowned and scratched their heads,

cudgelled their little brains

and ran around ...

… and *shouted*.

“What’s going on?”

“Stop shovin’ … Thingy!”

“It’s a puzzle to me!”

“And me!”

“And me!”

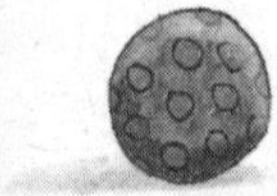

“Shoot, shoot!”

“I think –”*

“My name’s not ‘Thingy’!”

“It’s a mystery to me!”

“She’s a changed woman!”

"My theory is –"*

"Who wants a Prott?"

"It's a conundrum!"

"Foul, foul!"

"If you ask me –"*

"Goal!"

"An *enigma.*"

"… Thingy."

* More later (p293)

Meanwhile, Mrs Fritter stood

staring out of the staffroom window.

Spots of rain had begun to fall.

Mrs Fritter ... yes.

She was a changed woman, all right:

The rain was streaking the glass.

The face behind it seemed to waver

and dissolve,

and *shift its shape.*

Chapter 6

Look into My Eyes

Back at the house –

no bird seed to be found –

the bird was pecking

grumpily at a little bowl

of Crunchy Mice.

"They make Crunchy Canaries as well,"

said Horace.

"No, they don't," said the bird.

Later on the bird began

to complain about her cage.

"It's rubbish, this cage," she tweeted.

"Too small – too draughty,

and it needs a good clean."

Horace, meanwhile, had crouched down

on his tummy,

and was creeping out of the room.

"Come here," said the bird.

And she said, "Open this cage."

"No!" said Horace.

"You'll escape!

You'll get lost!

I'll get into trouble!

I'll..."

"Look into my eyes," said the bird.

So, anyway,

the bird sat in the window looking out

at the traffic, while Horace cleaned the cage.

"Put clean newspaper on the floor," said the bird.

"Fill the water bottle. Polish the mirror."

Horace had mixed feelings.

He disliked being bossed about

by a little bundle of feathers.

On the other hand (or paw),

the truth is, he admired the bird.

(And the goldfish,

by the way,

admired him.)

This bird is cleverer than Randolph,

thought Horace.

(Horace had met Randolph in an earlier story.)*

And he thought, I could learn a thing or two.

The bird, meanwhile,

was gazing back into the room.

She fluttered down, perched on Horace's head

and tweeted in his ear.

*The story of how they met is in this book, actually.
It's in *The Cat Who Got Carried Away*, page 163.

Chapter 7

Up and Away

Meanwhile, little Gary Gaskitt

– remember him? –

was *still* rolling away.

Well, up and away really.

Look what's happened

since we saw him last.

This is ridiculous, isn't it?

Whoever saw such a thing?

As fast as Gary is gaining weight

– 10lb 8oz now! –

his poor old father

is losing it.

That crane driver's no help either.

You'd think he'd spot

what's going on.

Instead of which, as you can see,

he's eating a sandwich,

listening to the radio,

waving to his girlfriend

on a passing bus,

rubbing his nose,

scratching his ear

and *looking the other way.*

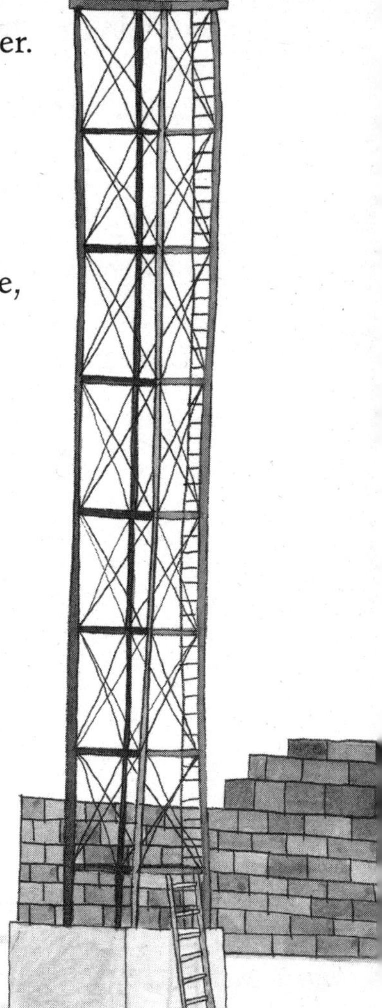

Chapter 8

Beethoven and Spinach

Back in the classroom

things were going from bad to worse.

Mrs Fritter lost her temper

over the slightest thing:

Her comments were

contradictory,

or sometimes just plain crazy.

Gus, Gloria and the others
could not tell
if they were coming or going.

In the afternoon for their music lesson
all they heard was Bach, Beethoven and Brahms.
And in home economics
all they cooked was spinach pie.

At the end of the day
Mr Blagg poked his head
round the classroom door,
flinched and disappeared again.
Randolph stayed out of sight altogether.
He smelled a rat too.

Till, at last – Yippee! – home-time.

Mrs Fritter, with a huge umbrella

in her hand and a wild look in her eye,

charged out of the classroom,

across the playground,

through the

school gates …

… and away.

Chapter 8 and a Bit

Meanwhile

I can't phone for a pizza –
I'm a cat!

Yes, you can.

No, I can't!

Yes, you can.

No, I can't!

Look into
my eyes ...

Yes, I can.

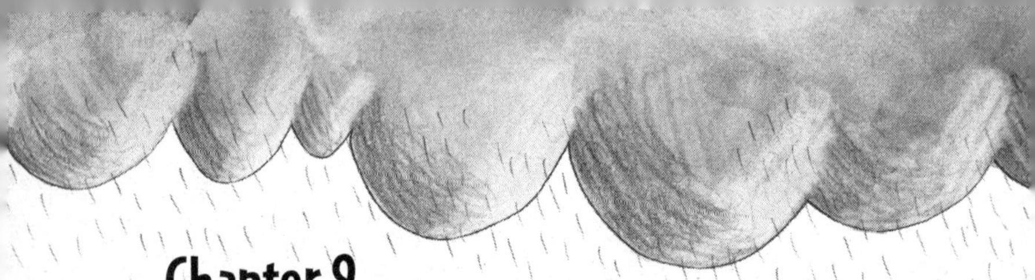

Chapter 9
The Face

It was a wet and gloomy afternoon.

Street lights were beginning to shine.

Cars had their headlights on.

A little gang of boys and girls came dodging and weaving along, in and out of shop doorways,

hiding behind wide ladies and phone boxes,

on the trail of a huge umbrella.

There was Gus and Gloria, of course (it's *their* book),

Molly and Tracey and Tom,

Rupert, Eric and Esmeralda.

Mrs Fritter marched down the High Street

in a straight line.

Large men and fierce-looking dogs

leapt out of her way.

Sensitive infants caught sight

of her wild gaze and burst into tears.

Gus, Gloria and the others stuck to the trail.

A left turn here. A right turn there.

A gate – a gravel path – a house.

The house was tall and dark.

Mrs Fritter climbed the front steps;

switched on the porch light.

The children in the shrubbery

crouched and watched.

They saw her open the door and step inside.

They saw her in the doorway

looking back into the street.

And they saw,

they really did,

at the very same time,

her *face,* all watery

and wavering

behind the glass –

one floor below! –

at the basement

window.

Chapter 10

In the Dungeon

Yes, phew!

Mrs Fritter's body

in the doorway.

Mrs Fritter's face at the window.

The children were astounded, astonished,

and – what's the word? – *flabbergasted*.

Well, no sooner had the front door

closed on Mrs Fritter No.1, than down

the basement steps they scrambled

to peer in through the barred

and dusty window at Mrs Fritter No.2.

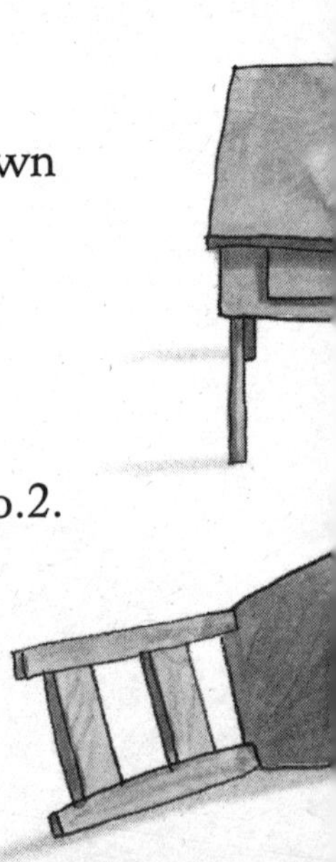

She was sitting on the floor with a broken chair beside her and a hopeful look in her eye.

The door was locked,

but Gloria found a key under the mat.

Once inside, the children took one look:

broken chair, fallen teacher –

sniffed one sniff: familiar perfume –

and guessed it all.

Of course, this was

the *real* Mrs Fritter.

The other one,

the mad imposter,

was…

"My *sister*, boys and girls,
here on a visit."
Mrs Fritter brushed a
cobweb from her hair.
"Gets funny turns
sometimes."
"Not that funny, Miss!"

"Anyway, she was a bit upset this morning,
and sort of tied me up
and locked me in down here.
I've only just got loose."

Well, the children were astounded

all over again,

astonished,

and – what's the word? – *affronted.*

"She's not your sister, Miss!" they cried.

"That's right!"

"No way!"

"She's your …

EVIL TWIN!*

*Which was actually what Gus had been trying to say back there (p271) in the playground. Fancy that!

Then,

just when things were going well,

and the rain had stopped,

and the sky was clear,

and a little bird (no, not that one)

was singing sweetly in the garden,

and the children were congratulating

themselves on a puzzle,

a *conundrum* solved ...

a shadowy figure

came down the basement steps

and slammed the door –

and locked it.

Chapter 11

Elsewhere ...

this was happening:

1. Horace

Horace had sneaked out of the room

while the bird was looking the other way.

He was halfway

to his friend's house,

taking a short cut

through somebody's garden

and, at that very moment,

only two doors away from

Mrs Fritter's house. Hm.

2. Mr Gaskitt (11st 9lb)

Mr Gaskitt – Puff, puff! –

was halfway up

a scaffold, while

2a. Little Gary

was halfway

down it.

3. The Bird

The bird was taking a bath

and singing sweetly.

Horace, under orders, had found the bath

and a few other things

in Gus and Gloria's toy cupboard.

The pizza was, for now, forgotten.

4. Mrs Gaskitt

Mrs Gaskitt –

not seen much of her lately,

have we? –

was rather busy,

also at that very moment,

with a tattooed lady and a man in a gorilla suit.

More later.

Chapter 12

Digging Like Mad!

Back in the basement the situation was ...Tricky!

The doors were locked, the windows barred.

The children's mobile phones were lost,

or left at home, or not charged up.

Their shouts – screams, even –

would never be heard on the faraway street.

And Mrs Fritter's evil twin

was out in the garden ... with a spade.

"Fond of gardening, she is," said Mrs Fritter.

But Gloria (on the table) saw things differently.

She's digging like mad, Miss!

Then Gus and the others began to protest.

They wanted a look, got it …

and wished they hadn't.

Chapter 12a: Horace the Hero

Now the basement door was heavy and thick

with great big hinges,

a massive lock … and a cat flap.

A cat flap. Hm.

Too small to escape through, of course.

Unless, that is, you were a…

Horace, at that very moment,

was making his way

along the garden wall to his friend's house.

And Horace was a cat, wasn't he?

He could do it.

Yes! Yippee! Hooray!

In through the cat flap.

Take a message in his collar.

(If he had a collar.)

Yes, Horace to

the rescue!

Horace the Hero!

He would love it,

wouldn't he?

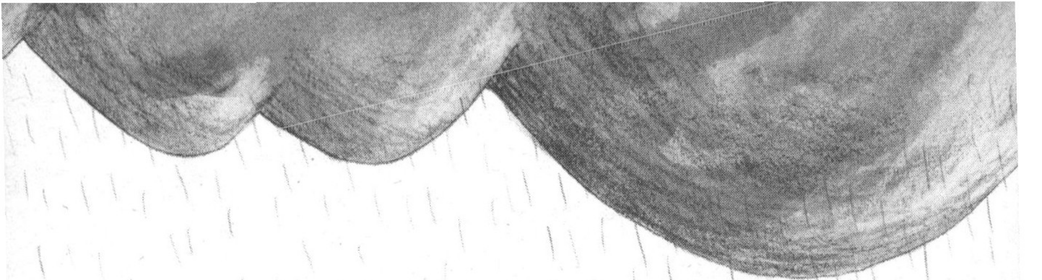

Only trouble was,

Horace never saw the faces at the window,

or heard the faint shouts from the house.

He was watching his step

on the slippery wall

(and that scary woman with the spade),

puzzling over the bossy bird,

thinking of all the things

he would tell his friend,

and *looking the other way.*

307

Chapter 12b: Tricky Situation No.2

As for little Gary, that teeny, tiny baby, that brave little bundle – look what's happening to him now.

He's up the creek and down the river. All at sea!

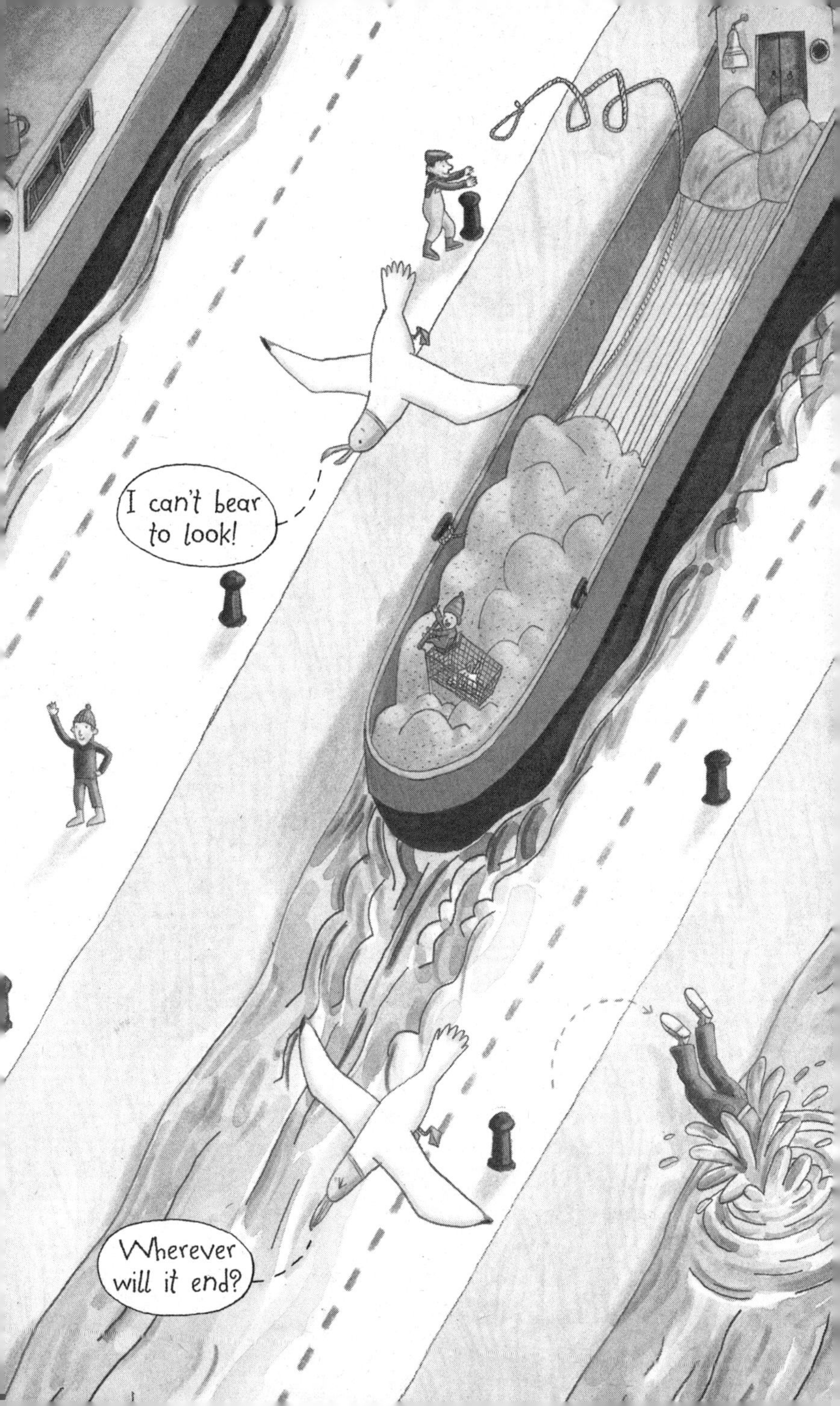
I can't bear to look!
Wherever will it end?

Chapters 13, 14 and 15

The Simplified Version

Meanwhile – Oh dear, tricky situation No.3 – we're running out of space. Only a few pages left and loads of words still to write. We'll have to squashtheminabit.

Or make 'em smaller. Can you read this at the back? This is too small, isn't it? And this is absolutely ridiculous. How about this? Better? Are you sure? Right – off we go.

So here we are. Back in the basement, Gus, Gloria and the others were scratching their heads and puzzling over how to escape. Out in the garden Mrs Fritter's evil twin had almost disappeared. The hole was deep and getting deeper. The sky was dark and getting darker. Rain was falling again … and Horace had given up on visiting his friend and was hurrying home. The bird, meanwhile, was fooling around in her little cage, with a mirror, and feeling lonely. Tweet, tweet! Meanwhile also, Mrs Gaskitt was having a tricky situation of her own with a man on stilts and a seal. Something to do with a circus. But that's another story. We'll have to skip it. This is the simplified version.*

Anyway – Puff, puff! – let's keep moving. There's thunder and lightning now. Mrs Fritter No.2 is banging around in the tool shed. What's she up to? What's going on? Look out, here she comes! Meanwhile, Horace is climbing in through his own cat flap, the little bird is reading the paper, and Mr Gaskitt is … swimming? Well Mrs Fritter No.2 is almost swimming.

*Actually, Mrs Gaskitt's story is ALSO in this book. It's in *The Woman Who Won Things*, paqe 83.

There's a torrent of rain out there … and – yes, here she comes – lit up in the lightning flashes – closer and closer – down the steps – the children can see her! – with a key in one hand – Mrs Gaskitt's taxi, by the way, has broken down and a great big hairy man is fixing it. Where were we? Yes, a key in one hand – CRASH! BANG! (lightning) – and – Oh, no! Oh, dear! Oh, my! – an axe in the other.

An axe. **An AXE**? Oops. Sorry about that.

"She looks a bit upset to me," said Mrs Fritter.

The children, Gus and Gloria, Molly and Tracey and Tom, Rupert, Eric and Esmeralda, agreed.

"She's got an axe, Miss!" they cried.

"She's got a *key*."

"Oh, mother…"

"She'll catch her death of cold out there," said Mrs Fritter. And now, the key is in the lock! The door is swinging open! 'The End' is near! Too near, actually. No room for pictures now – no space at all.

No, hoppit. Where were we? The End – yes. There she stands in the doorway, Mrs Fritter's evil twin, with a mad look in her eyes and an axe in her hand. Whereupon – who'd believe it? – another lady comes marching down the steps,

opens her mouth and,

"MARIGOLD, COME HERE!
PUT DOWN THAT AXE!
DON'T ARGUE!
LOOK INTO MY EYES!"

The children were amazed, of course, flabbergasted, it goes without saying, and delighted. Mrs Fritter seemed pleased too. "Chloe!" she cried. "What a pleasant surprise." And then the penny dropped. Oh, dear – no room to swing a cat even.

MIAOW?

We'll really have to squeeze this in. Sorry. Anyway, yes, the children took one look at this *familiar* lady No.3 …

… and guessed it all.

LETS!

Chapter 16

Happy Endings

1. The Bird and Horace

When Horace came home and found that teeny, tiny bird (lost and all alone) *reading the paper*, he admired her even more.

"Wish I was clever," he said.

"Wish I could read."

"No problemo," said the bird.

She fluttered up and perched on Horace's head.

"I'll teach you."

2. Mr Gaskitt and The Baby

Meanwhile, in a cafe

down by the docks,

little Gary Gaskitt: hair damp, eyes shut,

weight 10lb 3½oz,*

was safe and sound.

So was the shopping.

Mr Gaskitt was safe

and sound too, and

soaking wet,

of course.

And sleepy.

Sweet dreams,

Mr Gaskitt!

*Yes, 4½ oz lighter, minus one nappy – Poo!

3. Mrs Fritter and The Children

Back in the basement

Mrs Fritter No.2 had apologized

to Mrs Fritter No.1.

Mrs Fritter No.3 had given

Mrs Fritter No.1 a powerful hug

and taken Mrs Fritter No.2

home in her car.

Of course, their names

weren't *all* Mrs Fritter.

That would be silly, wouldn't it?

No, No.2 was Mrs Trotter

and No.3 was Mrs Molotovski.

So that sorts that out.

Meanwhile *now*, Mrs Fritter

– minus her alarming sisters –

is upstairs in the kitchen with Gus and Gloria,

Molly and Tracey and Tom,

Rupert, Eric and Esmeralda

eating *jelly and ice-cream*.

There wasn't supposed to *be* any jelly and

ice-cream – remember? – but never mind.

This *is* the happy ending after all.

Oh, yes, and finally...

4. Mrs Gaskitt and...

Meanwhile also,

Mrs Gaskitt had said goodbye to the circus

and was back in her taxi.

When she arrived home

she found a *parcel* on the back seat.

And when she picked it up,

Oh, no!

Oh, dear!

Oh, my!

the parcel went ...

Oink! *

*Fancy that.

Allan Ahlberg

is one of this country's most acclaimed and successful authors of children's books. He has won numerous awards including the Kurt Maschler Award in 1986, the Children's Book Award in 1987, the Blue Peter Book Award 2001 and the Children's Book Award: Books for Young Children 2002. His classic picture books include *Each Peach Pear Plum*, *Funnybones* and The Jolly Postman books illustrated by Janet Ahlberg, and *The Runaway Dinner, Previously* and *Under the Table* illustrated by Bruce Ingman.

Katharine McEwen

graduated from Kingston University in 1996 and has since illustrated around forty children's books for all ages. She is the illustrator of the picture books *Cows in the Kitchen*, *Hey, Tabby Cat!* and *Here Comes Tabby Cat*, *Send for a Superhero,* four Sam's Science books, the Silver Street series and the Gaskitt stories.